Cynthia d'Entremont

OAK ISLAND REVENGE

❧ a Jonah Morgan Mystery ❧

NIMBUS
PUBLISHING

Nimbus Publishing Limited
3731 Mackintosh St, Halifax, NS B3K 5A5
(902) 455-4286   nimbus.ca

Printed and bound in Canada

This novel is a work of fiction. Names, characters, places, and incidents are either the product of the author's imagination or are used fictitiously. Any resemblance to actual persons, living or dead, events or locales is entirely coincidental.

Author photo: Michelle Morgan
Design: Heather Bryan

Library and Archives Canada Cataloguing in Publication

D'Entremont, Cynthia
Oak Island revenge : a Jonah Morgan mystery / Cynthia d'Entremont.
ISBN 978-1-55109-899-9

I. Title.
PS8607.E676O23 2012   jC813'.6   C2011-907638-1

Nimbus Publishing acknowledges the financial support for its publishing activities from the Government of Canada through the Canada Book Fund (CBF) and the Canada Council for the Arts, and from the Province of Nova Scotia through the Department of Communities, Culture and Heritage.

This book was printed on Ancient-Forest Friendly paper

ANCIENT FOREST FRIENDLY™

MIX
Paper from responsible sources
FSC® C016245

For Joshua and Elianna

Where there is truth, there is freedom.
    ∾ the Wharf Prophet

CHAPTER 1

"YOU CAN FOOL THE WORLD, BUT YOU CAN'T fool the island," Sam Cooke muttered after artfully spraying his tobacco spittle on the wharf. "She'll right a multitude of wrongs," he added before sauntering off.

Jonah shuddered. It didn't matter that it was a mid-June Saturday afternoon and that the sun was triumphantly breaking through the Maritime clouds. The fog still clung in tendrils, grasping Oak Island in an air of gloom.

The darkness gripped Jonah as well, on account of Sam's casual words. The retired fisherman had forecasted many a storm and his gift for prophesying kept tongues wagging over cups of Red Rose tea all around Western Shore.

Why was the Wharf Prophet predicting the island's revenge?

Just that morning, Jonah's mom, Muriel, had blurted to a neighbour, "That Sam *knew* Dorothy was having a boy last week before it was even born."

"Humph," Ruth MacDonald had said dismissively. "There's a fifty-fifty chance of him guessing right."

Jonah's mother had paused, stirring an extra spoonful of honey into her tea before saying, "He predicted the weight. Right to the ounce. Dorothy's belly was barely the size of a turnip and Sam knew that baby would be nine pounds, ten ounces. Explain that, Mrs. Doubting Thomas."

Ruth had been speechless. As Jonah eavesdropped from the pantry, collecting a snack for his fishing expedition, he thought the event rivalled Moses parting the Red Sea.

Sitting on the wharf now, he bit into a gingersnap and smirked again at the memory of his mother besting her least favourite neighbour. Sam Cooke might be an unlikely prophet, dressed in rubber boots and chomping tobacco on the wharf, but Jonah's mother had managed to shut the flapping lips of Ruth MacDonald. It was a miracle!

But miracle or not, Jonah couldn't shake the hint of warning that Sam's words stirred.

For two hundred years Oak Island had lured fortune hunters nipped by the lust for Captain Kidd's treasure. Just three summers earlier, a posse of oilmen lugged their Texas-sized drilling rig over to the island in search of the Money Pit's secrets. For a time, they'd parked the rig in front of the Western Shore Fire Department. (Which was unlucky timing for Jonah's aunt and uncle in Martin's

Point. When their house caught fire, the rescue trucks were held hostage by the rig in front of the station's garage doors. Uncle David's house was left a pile of charred cinders and not one Texan said he was sorry.)

Eventually, like all of those who'd dug before, the oilmen gave up and carted their deadly rig back home.

But now, the start of summer in 1958, the island lay still. Too still. And no matter how many times the mothers of Western Shore gave the familiar caution, "Stay away from that darned place; it's riddled with holes," Jonah Morgan *knew* this would be the summer he'd finally sift the soil himself in search of gold.

Did the old fisherman somehow guess his plans?

Was Sam Cooke giving him a warning?

It was the secret right of every teenage boy spinning bicycle tires along the shoreline and drinking pop at the general store—the right to fling a shovel into the bottom of a rowboat and dream of pirated millions squirrelled away on the island shaded by oaks.

Really, fourteen was unusually old to be heading out on his first adventure to the island. He'd been ready last summer, he reasoned with himself now, but the memories of two summers before had still been too fresh. And his mother's leash too short…

He wasn't about to be reckless. He wouldn't go out on the water alone. Instead, Jonah would go with Beasley

Hodder. They shared a birthday, he and Beaz—April Fools' Day. Not born in the same place, though. Like most newborns in Western Shore in the mid-forties, Jonah bellowed his first cry in his parents' house overlooking the salty waters of the Atlantic.

Beaz, on the other hand, arrived in antiseptic style at the Grace Maternity Hospital in Halifax. Other than that, they'd grown up climbing the same trees, fishing off the same wharf, and combing the same beach in search of treasure.

Never out to the island, though. Beaz had a strict mother with an uncanny pair of eyes in the back of her head—or a healthy network of nosy neighbours. The previous summer, the two boys had never gotten too far out of sight before some busybody was herding them back toward home.

And Jonah suspected his own mother was a part of that network. She wanted—no, *needed*—to know where he was constantly. He'd given her last summer freely, especially around the anniversary of Caleb's death.

Just this spring he and Beaz had ridden their bikes all the way to Martin's River before Beaz's mother came chugging along in the family Ford. Beaz had had trouble sitting on the wharf the next day. Along with an extra set of eyes, Mrs. Hodder wielded a strap with a right arm muscled from years of baking extra bread to sell at the general store.

Jonah's punishment came in the form of a heaping plate of peanut butter cookies—tangible evidence of his mother's worrying. Did his mother guess the consequences Beaz faced for his discovered wanderings? Did she suspect that Mrs. Hodder didn't beat just butter and flour?

"Got any bait?" Beaz yelled a moment later, as he whizzed down the wharf on his bicycle, a fishing rod bouncing above his head.

"Of course I do!" Jonah shouted back. "You think I'm sittin' here for the fun of it?" He wondered what new chore Mrs. Hodder had invented this afternoon to keep Beaz from arriving in time to catch the highest tide.

"Maybe." Beaz grinned. His two front teeth stuck out a bit—not enough to call him buck-toothed, but enough to make you take a second look when he dispensed his words of wisdom. *Pearls,* he called them—the wisecracks, *not* the teeth.

"Is she still leaving next week?" Jonah heard the quiver in his own voice. He didn't mean to sound so…scared.

No matter how many licks of the strap Beaz supposedly got, he always managed to laugh like life was one big trip to the circus. "Yup. She's leaving on Wednesday."

"And school's finished on Thursday afternoon." Jonah sighed. The minute Beaz had announced last week that his mother was spending the summer caring for her ailing mother in Halifax, the boys had begun planning their island escape.

They both had chores to complete in the early mornings and then they were free to roam for the rest of the day. Really free, thanks to Beaz's grandmother's weak heart. Hopefully Mrs. Hodder wouldn't be able to trace their wayward steps from her temporary home on Quinn Street in Halifax. And as long as Jonah kept his own mother off their trail, they'd be golden.

"Last night she tried to talk Dad into letting me go with her." Beaz gave a nervous laugh.

Jonah's grip loosened and the fishing rod slipped from his hands into the waves lapping against the wharf. "Dang!" He stripped off his shirt and dove into the seaweed to rescue his prized possession—a store-bought reel. "Got it," he shouted, flinging the rod toward Beaz with one hand while wiping the slimy sea grass with the other.

"Little jumpy?" Beaz roared with laughter.

Gripping the weathered ladder, Jonah flicked a glob of seaweed at Beaz. He flopped back up onto the splintery boards and narrowed his eyes. "*Not* funny."

"I don't know what you're so worried about," Beaz said. "It's not *your* hide she'll tan if she finds out we've been digging on that 'death trap' of an island."

If Jonah hadn't known Beaz, those words would have sounded ridiculous—what fourteen-year-old kid in his right mind was afraid of getting whooped by his mother?

Teeth chattering, he tugged his shirt over his head. Even in the hot sun with a dry shirt on, he shivered. *It's the chill of the wind from the shifting tide*, he told himself. Not the new sound that wafted from a distance—Sam Cooke's morbid whistle.

Taps.

A song to remember the dead.

CHAPTER 2

CHARLOTTE BARKHOUSE ALWAYS HIKED HER skirts up a little shorter than the other girls. Not enough to catch it from her mother, but enough to get noticed by the grade nine boys. She also wore nylons with perfectly straight seams up the back—never out of place.

Girls lost their minds and started chasing boys in grade six, but the boys held out until about halfway through grade eight. Now that it was the end of the year, Charlotte had the attention of males in both grades eight and nine.

Jonah sat at the end of the grade eight row, still not willing to admit that he had lost any of his marbles when it came to girls. Even so, their one-room schoolhouse smelled different on this last day before summer, partly from the rosewater scent drifting like a noxious gas from Charlotte's direction. And partly something else, something stronger, more pleasant—the air of anticipated freedom.

"We still have a full day of learning left," Mr. Steevens warned the thirty-four restless students from grades primary to nine. His frozen frown relaxed almost into a smile when he answered Charlotte's hand. "Yes?"

"May I read a poem?"

"Of course," the teacher replied, grinning at the grade nine girl in a manner that made Jonah's stomach queasy. Maybe grade eight and nine boys weren't the only ones who noticed Charlotte.

With her usual dramatic bounce, Charlotte stepped to the front of the class and cleared her throat, tugging at the gold locket around her neck. At sixteen, she was a year late leaving grade nine thanks to a childhood bout of scarlet fever.

Fellow older grade nine student, Marshall Delray, gave a low admiring whistle and Mr. Steevens' cheeks flamed like red Smarties. "Shhh!" he hissed.

"In honour of our last day *ever* in our beloved Western Shore School, I've selected a poem, 'A Thought From a Lonely Death Bed,' by Elizabeth Barrett Browning." She began reading, "'If God compel thee to this destiny, To die alone, with none beside thy bed…'" She ended with the words, "'But stoop Thyself to gather my life's rose, And smile away my mortal to Divine!'"

The room was silent.

"Um, interesting choice of poem," Mr. Steevens stuttered.

"Thank you, dear."

Beaz jabbed Jonah in the ribs. "He called her 'dear,'" he whispered, grinning.

Jonah couldn't blame Beaz for his bubbling joy in the midst of an ode to the death of a one-room schoolhouse. Beaz's emancipation had been jump-started yesterday when he waved an outwardly solemn farewell to his mother.

This morning, the furrows in Beaz's brow had smoothed and he no longer twitched at sudden loud noises. Although he mostly used to claim to be startled for comedic purposes, Jonah had occasionally spotted an instant of naked fear before his friend's blue eyes blinked into merriment. Now Beaz was as cool as a cucumber and it was Jonah's turn to have a stomach cinched in knots.

He stared up at the wooden-raftered belly of what had been his prison for ten months of the year since he was five years old. Charlotte's honed voice had brought a swift death to today's celebration.

In September, he and the other younger students would all go to the new Gold River–Western Shore Consolidated School that was opening its doors down the road. Jonah resented Charlotte's reminder that the two months of summer would whiz by in a blink. He also resented the loss of something else—the feeling of being cocooned in a place that felt familiar. Safe.

At the end of the day, Mr. Steevens passed out their

grading cards and lifted the cowbell on his desk to give one final ring of dismissal.

"Summer!" Beaz yelped, jumping up at least two feet in the air.

"Summer," Jonah echoed, allowing the joy from the morning to seep back into his bones. He emerged from the schoolhouse and dragged Beaz by the elbow. "Let's make sure the *Gingerale*'s patch is holding."

They tore down the hill on their bikes toward Vaughn Road and then veered left into their secret hideaway in a little patch of forest off the beaten track. Jonah pulled the tarp back off the hull of the *Gingerale* and stared at their very own salvaged rowboat with mismatched oars.

He and Beaz had scraped, patched, and sanded the dubious vessel until it showed signs of becoming shipshape. Secretly, Jonah imagined that he was getting his first Chevy roadworthy. Then he'd remind himself to be content with this summer's accomplishment. Beaz's mother's strap may have left an occasional welt, but Jonah's family carried deeper wounds—wounds that would keep Jonah's desire for motorized independence in check at least until he graduated from high school. Maybe even college.

Together, it took Jonah and Beaz about fifteen minutes to half drag, half carry the paint-chipped vessel down to the shore. "We've got to find a closer hiding spot," Jonah panted, wiping beads of sweat with the back of his sleeve. "At this rate, neither one of us will have enough pep to row over to Oak Island and back every day. And we don't even know if she's seaworthy yet."

"She floated the last time," Beaz said, emptying the contents from his lunch pail. "Only needed this at the end."

Staring at Beaz's tin pail that doubled as a bailing pan, Jonah remembered the two peanut butter cookies left over in his own lunch. "Dang!" he muttered. "Forgot my lunch pail at school."

"Just get it tomorrow. Your mother won't care." Beaz sighed. "I think for every whippin' I get, your mother bakes two dozen cookies for you."

"Uh, Beaz?"

"Yep?"

"There's no school tomorrow."

"Oh yeah."

Jonah's stomach growled. "I'm gonna have to go back for it now before Mr. Steevens locks up. We'll need to take our lunch pails with us when we treasure hunt."

Despite the crimp in the beginning of summer festivities, Jonah whistled happily all the way back to the schoolhouse—at least until he reached the general store.

"Come here, kid!" Marshall Delray called out from the stoop.

Jonah slammed on his brakes and skidded in the gravel.

He couldn't help but turn around just to check. *Ten feet for sure!* It was his own best skid record and there was no one around to brag to. He glanced at Marshall's sweaty red face and mussed shirt open at his bare, sunburned neck—nope, not a soul who'd care.

"Where you going, kid?"

Wondering what he'd done to earn the seventeen-year-old's unwelcome attention, Jonah answered truthfully, "Forgot my lunch pail at school."

Marshall nodded. "Good. Take this and give it to the teacher, will ya? But don't tell him who it's from. You know, anon...anona..."

"Anonymous?"

"Yeah." Marshall glared. "And don't read it!"

What Marshall wanted, Marshall got. That was the first rule kids growing up in Western Shore learned if they were to survive without fear of a weekly thrashing in the rosebushes behind the schoolhouse. So far, Jonah had stayed off Marshall's radar.

"Sure," Jonah said, taking the folded stub of paper. He prayed Mr. Steevens was still at the school. After all, class had let out almost an hour ago—how long did a teacher of thirty-four children in grades primary to nine hang around on the last day of the year?

Pedalling toward the school, he felt the heat from Marshall's glare sear his back more than the afternoon sun beating down on him. He didn't want to return past the general store later having failed to deliver.

When he rounded the bend, he saw Mr. Steevens' 1955 baby blue Pontiac parked in the school parking lot—a welcome sight. Jonah slowed down and caught his breath.

Once he'd propped his bike up against the bushes, he took the note from his pocket. Now that he was here in time, the initial fear of failure fled. Instantly, it was replaced with something else—curiosity. What kind of note would Marshall Delray be writing to the teacher? *Thanks for helping me pass grade nine in just two years?*

Jonah looked over his shoulder. Twice. Then he went around the far side of the school, just to be sure that the coast was clear. Hidden from the road, he silently opened the paper—as if he was surreptitiously trying to get the wrapper off a stick of gum in church.

The note wasn't very long, or very informative:

CHAPTER 3

ANONYMOUS. A NINE-LETTER WORD MEANING Marshall Delray was a chicken-livered blackmailer. And now Jonah was the messenger! It must be his name—Jonah. He was doomed since Bible days to be the reluctant bearer of unpopular news.

A honeybee buzzed in the wild rosebushes as sweat dripped down his forehead and stung his eyes. How could he deliver Marshall's note to Mr. Steevens and pretend not to know what was in it?

He couldn't. Not in person.

The driver's window on Mr. Steevens' Pontiac was open. Without thinking about his own chicken-liveredness, Jonah reached in and placed the note on the steering wheel. He whipped his hand out and backed away from the baby blue beast, as if expecting it to swallow him whole and carry him off to a faraway land.

It felt as though every eyeball in Western Shore was locked on him, watching.

Glancing around, he saw and heard no one—only his own conscience whispering that he was now tangled up in something shadowed and vile.

He wasn't hungry anymore but he knew he still had to face Mr. Steevens and collect his lunch pail. Eventually the knots in his stomach would unravel and when they did, those cookies would hit the spot. Besides, Beaz was waiting back at the shore.

The door to the schoolhouse was ajar enough for Jonah to slip quietly into the entryway by the coat rack. Thankfully, the inside door to the schoolroom was shut and his pail sat harmlessly waiting on the shelf above his hook. If he was lucky, he'd get in and out without his teacher even knowing he'd been back.

He held his breath, reached out his arm, and stopped—

A noise.

A book falling to the floor?

Then voices drifted from inside the schoolroom behind the closed door.

A man's voice. *Mr. Steevens.*

Another voice. *A woman? A girl?*

I know about YOU and HER, Marshall's note had accused.

Did the voice belong to that *HER*?

Jonah wrapped his fingers around the handle of his lunchbox. He didn't want to know or think anything more about Mr. Steevens, or Marshall, or *HER*. He just wanted to collect his lunchbox and hightail it back to the *Gingerale* and Beaz. The only secrets he wanted to learn about were the ones buried long ago on Oak Island.

Please don't creak, he silently begged his tin lunch pail.

It obeyed.

But the schoolhouse front door, swinging on rusty hinges, did not. Prompted by a hot gust of wind, the front door groaned and squeaked and finally slammed with a forceful thud.

"Who's there?" Mr. Steevens shouted, his voice sounding nervous.

Guilty.

Jonah froze. *Now what?* He looked for a place to hide and spotted the drapes on the window. Would they conceal him? Or should he stay here and say something? After all, he didn't do anything wrong, right?

"I should go," the girl said.

What if Mr. Steevens sees me and guesses I left the note? Jonah thought. Then he had a more terrifying thought. *What if Mr. Steevens thinks I wrote the note?*

Say nothing, Jonah decided. He slipped behind the heavy musty fabric and held his breath as Mr. Steevens' footsteps grew louder. Lighter footsteps trailed behind the teacher's brisk stride.

"There's no one here," the teacher said, sighing only a few feet from where Jonah hid. "It's only the wind. That door never latches properly. This place is a dump. They finally build a new school and I'm not even going to be around to enjoy it."

"I need to go home," the girl said.

"Comb your hair first," Mr. Steevens said. "Straighten yourself up a bit and then I'll drive you."

"What if someone sees you?"

"I'm your teacher. Why shouldn't I drop you off?"

Listening to the sound of water splashing from the broom closet at the other end of the entry, Jonah figured it was noisy enough for him to gulp a few gasps of dusty air behind the curtain. His head spun and his leg muscles wilted. Licking his lips, he imagined slurping an ice-cold bottle of pop from the general store. He even had seven cents in his pocket.

But first he'd have to get past Marshall standing guard like a bulldog.

"Let's go, dear," Mr. Steevens said, opening the creaking front door and then slamming it shut. Twice.

Jonah listened to the padlock click into place and slid out from behind the curtain. *Who was with the teacher?* he wondered, a suspicion growing. The voice was oddly familiar, but different—nervous?

Moving the maroon drape just a smidge, he peered out the window to see Mr. Steevens open the car door for Charlotte Barkhouse.

Bingo.

And even though Jonah tried to convince himself that he hadn't completely lost his marbles over girls, he knew something wasn't quite right about his classmate.

For starters, there was dirt smudged on the back of her sweater. And then there was the way one of the seams in her nylons zigzagged like it couldn't make up its mind which direction to go. And there was something else too, something that nagged at him without really announcing itself. Like when someone got a haircut, or new glasses— you knew there was a difference but couldn't put your finger on it right away.

He watched Mr. Steevens pick up the slip of paper and read the note. Then the teacher thrust the key into the ignition and ground the baby blue beast into gear.

Gravel spit out from the spinning tires and the car tore off down the road. If Mr. Steevens didn't slow down soon, Charlotte would have to throw herself from a moving vehicle to land on her doorstep—her house was just around the next bend, a stone's throw from the general store.

Jonah leaned against the wall and slid down to the planked floor. How would he get out of here?

First things first, he ate *both* the cookies in his lunch box. Beaz was on his own for a snack, he thought with a twinge of guilt as he licked the crumbs from cookie number two. Funny, ten minutes ago Jonah had thought he'd never eat again. Now he'd downed two cookies and still felt like his ribs were hollow.

Then he got up and scooped the tin cup into the bucket of water on the narrow shelf in the broom closet. The basin beside it was the makeshift "sink" for washing up after a visit to the outside toilet. The bucket was the "water cooler" and everyone shared the same tin cup along with the latest influenza bug.

The new Gold River school would have indoor toilets, sinks, and drinking fountains. Visiting the "facilities" on a cold winter's day would be a heck of a lot more pleasant for students the next school year.

Jonah wouldn't have minded some of that wintry chill today, though. He gulped a second cupful of water. The cool breeze from the tiny open window didn't give much relief from the stifling heat. Another bee buzzed, hovering by the windowsill, threatening to drift in and torment him in his prison.

The window had no screen.

With his lunch pail dangling under his arm like a fat purse, Jonah balanced on an upside-down mop bucket. He gripped the windowsill and sprung up to the twenty-by-twelve-inch opening. Shinnying headfirst, he landed in one of the wild rosebushes that flourished around the schoolhouse.

Staring up at the sky while thorns and branches dug into his flesh, Jonah realized then and there what else had been different about Charlotte.

Her skirt—it was longer.

CHAPTER 4

"You're up to something," Jonah's mom said the next morning, eying the mountain of food that was growing on the kitchen counter.

Jonah held his breath. His mother had watched him like a hawk last summer, pummelling him with questions and commands: *Where are you going? Stay off the pavement when you're on your bike! Swimming? Not without adult supervision. Just wait. Let me get my hat...*

He'd hoped enough time had passed and that this summer would be different. So far, he'd amassed one half-dozen gingersnaps, three apples, four peanut butter sandwiches, and some day-old tea biscuits.

"Leave him alone, Muriel. He's fourteen. You don't have to hover over him like a mother hen."

Jonah crammed some of the food into his lunch pail and shoved the overflow into his knapsack. He crossed his fingers, hoping that it was the end of his mother's interrogation.

It wasn't.

"You're not going up the Gold River to Kill Devils, are you?" his mother asked.

Armed with the truth, Jonah stared her in the eye. "Wouldn't think of it."

"You know that's where Jimmy Morash broke his neck."

"For heaven's sake, Muriel, that was twenty years ago. And Jimmy was his own special brand of hellion."

"Well, it still bears repeating," she said, flicking the breadcrumbs off the counter into her hand. "No son of mine is going to risk life and limb just to have the bragging rights of diving from that cliff. And stay off the pavement when you're riding on the highway. And don't go swimming without an adult. And don't even think about going to that island—"

Beaz interrupted her warning and saved Jonah from being forced to tell a lie by banging on the screen door in the nick of time. "Anybody home?"

"Come in!" Jonah shouted. "I'm ready to go."

Charging through the door, Beaz slung his knapsack onto the table. "Got enough food for the whole day?"

Jonah's mom frowned. "Where is it you boys are off to?"

The phone rang.

Saved again!

"Hello," his mother said into the phone, and then, putting her hand over the mouthpiece, she whispered,

"Don't you two leave until I'm done with my call. I told Beaz's mother that I'd watch out for both of you."

Not saved!

"Oh no!" she said, after listening for a moment.

Jonah recognized the muffled high-pitched shriek of Ruth MacDonald's voice boomeranging around the kitchen. He couldn't hear clearly, but "scandalous" was used at least once and he was sure "outrageous" sliced through the airwaves three times.

"When?" his mom asked, finally, after Ruth appeared to have paused for a breath.

More shrieking erupted and finally his mom said goodbye.

"What are you boys standing around here for?" she said, waving her arms. "Go on, get out of here! I need to talk to your father…"

Shrugging at Beaz, Jonah grabbed his knapsack and the boys jumped on their bikes.

"Like shooting fish in a barrel," Beaz sang out as they whizzed past the general store.

Instinctively Jonah glanced at the stoop. No Marshall. The over-aged grade nine student hadn't been there yesterday afternoon, either, when Jonah had pedalled pell-mell back from the schoolhouse to the beach. And like yesterday, Jonah's insides relaxed when he realized he wasn't in for another encounter with Superstupid.

"Yeah," Jonah said. "Mrs. MacDonald must have had a truckload of gossip for Mom to be so distracted. It's like she didn't even care about us anymore." He jammed on his brakes and skidded out in the dirt. "Which works for me."

Beaz stopped too. "Where are you going?"

"The store. I want to buy a pop for lunch."

They backtracked to the general store and each picked out a bottle of pop from the refrigerator. Jonah raised his eyebrows when he noticed Beaz's dime.

"Dad let me have some of the egg money," Beaz explained when he collected his three cents change.

Jonah shrugged. They'd been best friends since grade primary, but he still didn't quite understand how Beaz's family worked. His dad was so kind, and his mother so—not.

"Where are you boys off to today?" Betty Schofield asked, clicking her gum behind ruby-red lips. Mrs. Schofield owned the store, ran the mail, and fixed her own roof—all in stilt-like high heels. She was even rumoured to fertilize her vegetable garden in pumps. Green ones.

Staring at her fingers for a minute, Jonah wondered if the woman had already sifted Oak Island from stem to stern and claimed Captain Kidd's treasure for herself. Her hands dripped with at least twenty rings set with flashy stones and she only had ten fingers. He double-checked just to be sure. *Yup, ten fingers—some with two or three rings apiece.*

He spent so long counting Mrs. Schofield's fingers and rings that Beaz was forced to answer her.

"We're going beachcombing," he said evasively. "May I use your bathroom, please?"

She glared at them both, up and down, spending an extra long time looking at Jonah's hands. He curled his dirty fingernails into his palm.

"The outhouse is around back," she said dismissively, and reached to answer her jingling phone.

Beaz did his business and rejoined Jonah in the parking lot by their bikes. "Funny," he said.

"What?"

"She said there was toilet paper out there, but all I saw was the Simpsons-Sears catalogue. Do you think that was for wipin' or readin'?"

Jonah rolled his eyes. "Ruth MacDonald says Mrs. Schofield's so cheap she only pays Sally a nickel to scrub her floors, so I guess she wouldn't share real, honest-to-Pete TP with the likes of us."

"It's a good thing, then."

"What is?" Jonah asked, flinging his leg over his bicycle.

"That I didn't need any."

Grinning, the boys pedalled toward Martin's Point and turned off the highway at Vaughn Road. They found the *Gingerale* snug in her new hiding spot behind a clump of bushes near the shoreline. Stashing their bikes, they carried the rowboat over the rocks to the edge of the water.

Jonah inhaled the salt air. Even though he had lived next to the water all his life, he had never grown accustomed to it—he could still taste the ocean in every breath. Caleb used to love the water too. "Swims like a fish," their dad would say.

Caleb had been the best at a lot of things: swimming, baseball, composition, geometry, rebuilding engines…

Jonah still felt like he was stumbling through life blindfolded, hoping to find his way toward something meaningful. This summer, Oak Island would belong to him alone. Would this turn out to be what he was best at—treasure hunting?

Staring at the island, Jonah swallowed his memories. "There's no fog today," he announced, as if that would dispel the cloud that seemed to loom in spite of the blazing sun.

"Groovy," Beaz said.

Breathing more deeply, Jonah shut his eyes. Just a week ago, when he'd learned Beaz's mother was going AWOL, he'd relaxed. After two years, Jonah finally felt like he'd freed himself from the ache in his stomach that had first appeared the day his brother's car had crashed. But that was before Sam Cooke's eerie prophecy. Now something had changed. The ache was back. And Jonah couldn't quite figure out why.

CHAPTER 5

"IT'D BE LESS ROWIN' IF WE STASHED THE BOAT down Crandall's Point Road," Beaz said, wiping sweat off his face.

Glancing across the waves, Jonah replied, "Harder to find a good hiding spot for the boat, though. There aren't as many trees close to the shore. Besides, we'd have to bike further to get there."

"But we'd be hidden from the spies when we rowed."

Jonah glanced at the hilly treed landscape back from the way they'd come. It didn't take much convincing to believe all eyes were focused on them—just the hint of someone watching made him feel like he was a bug squished under a microscope. "We should be wearing life jackets," he said, his conscience prickling like quills on a perturbed porcupine. If his mother ever found out—

"What if someone sees us?" Beaz shivered. "Bad enough you're on the water, your mother's just scared something will happen to you. My mother's the opposite, she's the one that'll do the killin'."

Beaz was the kind of kid that the tellin' was ten times better than the bein', meaning Jonah had known his friend to exaggerate a story enough to make it interesting. That's probably what he did with his mother—after all, Jonah had never actually *seen* her hit Beaz. Not even once. Did he just talk about his mother that way to be funny?

"Hurry up!" Jonah said. "Duck your head and row to the island's South Shore Cove. Then we'll be out of sight before we beach the boat. If anyone notices it before then, they'll think we're just fishing."

"Maybe we should bring our rods next time," Beaz said, his protruding teeth sparkling in the sunlight.

It didn't take long to paddle around to the far side of island. The waves quietly lapped at the boat, not putting up much of a fight for the amateur rowers—there wasn't even a hint of a breeze. Soon, the bottom of the boat scraped against the moss-covered rocks lurking beneath the surface.

Jonah splashed into the knee-deep water and tugged the boat ashore. "It's quiet," he whispered. There was no reason for it, the whispering. At least none he could explain without sounding like a sissy.

Beaz must have sensed something too. "They say there are ghosts on the island. Ghosts of the slaves who were murdered after constructing the booby traps to bury the treasure." He whipped his index finger across his throat, making a slicing sound. "Captain Kidd didn't want anyone spillin' the beans about his loot."

The leaves rustled.

"What's that?" Beaz hissed.

Jonah gulped. "The wind."

"There is no wind."

"I know."

"I don't see any oak trees."

"Me neither."

They stood together, shoulder to shoulder, both frozen and staring up at the dense forest towering in front of them. Jonah remembered what he'd heard spoken around Western Shore since birth—the legend that Oak Island treasure would not be found until there were no more oak trees alive on the island. Were all of the oaks gone now? His heart thudded.

"We're here," Beaz said.

"Yup, we sure are."

"Now what?"

"Not a clue," Jonah said, then changed his mind. "I guess we tie up the *Gingerale* and find the Money Pit. I heard it's not far from this cove."

"Where'd you hear that?"

"From a big, super-stupid pain in the neck. Three guesses and the first two don't count."

Rolling his eyes, Beaz mumbled, "Marshall."

"Remember two summers ago when he was bragging one day about the gold chain he found in the Money Pit?"

"Do you think he comes here a lot?" Beaz's eyes widened.

Ghosts were one thing, Jonah thought, understanding Beaz's alarm. You could hold out hope that a ghost was just a spooky legend—but Marshall Delray was as real as the end of your bloody nose if you got in his way.

"Relax, Beaz. I heard he's working at the Chester gas station six days a week starting today." For once he was thankful for Ruth MacDonald's ever-yapping lips. In Western Shore, eavesdropping was the only sure way to find out what parents *and* bullies were up to.

"Do you think anyone else comes here?"

Jonah shrugged. In all the planning and scheming he'd never really spent time thinking about that. "I guess it's possible." He considered the other older boys at school. "If Marshall's working, that only really leaves John and Jacob Plant. It's not like any *girls* are going to bother."

Beaz sighed like a truckload of gravel had just rolled off his shoulders. "I saw them pack up this morning. John and Jacob. They're going to work on their uncle's farm in New Brunswick—all summer."

"So I guess we're golden. There are a couple kids in Martin's Point but even if they show up here, why would they blab? No one's really *supposed* to be here on account of the danger."

"Like hidden underground tunnels caving in." Beaz's shoulders sagged again.

"If Marshall is smart enough to survive Oak Island, so are we."

Heading east, Jonah led the way in search of the Money Pit. Loads of expeditions had tried and failed to find the true secret of the island. He wasn't sure why he felt the need to hunt when so many others had given up. The thought of treasure had lured men for generations and had even claimed some lives in the process.

"Holy hillbilly!" Beaz whistled when they entered a clearing.

"Looks like a bunch of overgrown Lincoln Logs," Jonah said, surveying the two shafts now known as the Money Pit. Boards and beams in various stages of decay were scattered about. "I wonder which shaft Hedden dug and which one is Chappell's?" He poked at the dirt with his shovel. Bits of crusty soil spilled down into the hole, disappearing into the darkness.

"Maybe we should bring some rope next time."

Nodding, Jonah jabbed at more dirt. Treasure hunters had searched and sifted the Money Pit—pouring away their dollars and gleaning nothing in return. "And a light."

Beaz frowned. "A lot of people have dug here already—"

Jonah read Beaz's unspoken thoughts: *And if they didn't find anything, how can we?*

"We'll dig some more," Jonah said. "And we'll sift through the piles of dirt over there. Maybe someone missed coins and stuff the first time. I think that's how Marshall found the chain."

"Maybe," Beaz mumbled, frowning.

"There's got to be something up for grabs," Jonah encouraged. "And hey, if we come up with nothin' here, we'll look around the island for other places the treasure could be buried. Mr. Steevens said something about a theory that the Money Pit was a decoy. It'll be a piece of cake."

"Piece of cake," Beaz repeated. But his frown stayed put, like the whole ordeal would be anything but simple.

Staring into the bottomless black in front of him, Jonah licked his dry lips. Sometimes he needed a minute to think.

And a bottle of pop.

"Let's eat now," Jonah said, prying open his overflowing lunch pail. In a flash, the squeak of the hinge yanked his memory back to hiding behind the curtain in the schoolhouse yesterday afternoon—when the minutes had lagged by like an eternity.

Beaz gnawed hungrily on a boiled egg.

And Jonah realized that he still hadn't said a word to his friend about seeing Mr. Steevens and Charlotte together.

Or Marshall's note.

Jonah guzzled his drink and watched Beaz sip his pop with a joyful grin—like a wayward puppy that'd been let off the leash and roamed too far from its owner.

She really beats him, Jonah decided then and there. In this moment he'd caught a naked glimpse behind Beaz's smile and deep down he knew there were secrets that even best friends didn't share. Ones that made nightmares seem more real.

"What's that?" Beaz pointed to a brown furry mound on the beam across the shaft.

Scurrying around, Jonah inched toward the silent creature. "A rabbit," he whispered.

"Why's it just lying there?"

Leaning closer, Jonah spoke over the buzz of the gathering flies. "It's dead."

"Creepy."

"Um, hmm…" Jonah's eyes had moved past the rabbit carcass to where letters were carved into the beam.

CALEB

CHAPTER 6

Caleb was here. The thought scraped, like picking a scab off an old wound. Oak Island wouldn't belong only to him and Beaz. "The rabbit was caught in a snare," he said aloud, turning away from the rotting carcass. His appetite for treasure hunting faltered.

"A dead rabbit? Seems like bad luck," Beaz said. He collected the remains of his lunch, nervously wiping his mouth.

And who set the snare? Jonah kept the thought to himself. Caleb's name mocked him. "The wire's rusty," Jonah said. "Probably an old snare from years ago." He grabbed two sticks and prodded the rabbit's carcass away from the Money Pit. "Let's start digging."

They sifted through mounds of grass-covered dirt until their arms were rubbery and their water jugs were empty. Finally, the two boys called it a day and piled into the *Gingerale,* rowing back to the mainland.

"I wonder what *that's* all about," Jonah said, skidding his bike to a stop.

Dozens of cars filled the parking lot and snaked down the road. Other than weddings, funerals, and Sunday services, all community gatherings occurred in the jam-packed one-room schoolhouse. Once the new Gold River school opened for business, this building would officially become known as "The Western Shore Community Centre."

"A community meetin'? Now?" Beaz shook his head. "It's not like there's a potluck supper…"

Jonah's stomach growled. "Better go in and see what's going on," he said reluctantly. He knew his mom would have something tasty concocted in the kitchen and he wanted to poke around in Caleb's room a bit and see if there was any evidence of his brother's excursion to Oak Island—one Jonah had never known about.

But a packed schoolhouse at five o'clock *was* worth investigating.

Betty Schofield teetered on her cherry-red heels at the front of the room as she chaired the meeting, her permed hair teased extra high. "It's scandalous," the makeshift mayor said, flinging her arms in the air as she gripped a piece of paper. "We've never had such a thing happen in Western Shore."

Nobody had elected her. Western Shore didn't need a mayor, with its handful of roads and slightly bigger fistful of houses dropped along the highway. Betty just took over at meetings. And everybody let her. After all, she was a successful business*woman*—a legend from Chester to Martin's River. Rumour had it that she'd even signed up to drive her Ford down to Martin's Point as the "school bus" when the new school opened in Gold River.

Ruth MacDonald stood. "I always said he'd be trouble. The board should've never hired a foreigner."

"Land sakes, Ruth. He's no foreigner! Ontario *is* a part of Canada, you know," Jonah's mother said.

In spite of his growing dread that something awful had happened, Jonah smirked at his mother's feisty retort. *Way to go, Mom!* She really was showing signs of getting back her former spunk.

Jonah's dad cleared his throat. Because he was the community's only lawyer, people often waited to get his two cents' worth on things. "It seems to me," Abraham Morgan said, "that we have a couple of things going on that may or may not be related. The first is that our teacher has resigned and won't be back in the fall."

Betty waved the sheet of paper again. "Dated yesterday and left in the outgoing mailbox before I woke up this morning."

"Addressed to you?" someone called from the crowd.

With her cheeks heating up as red as her lips and shoes, Betty mumbled something about being on the school board and that as such, she was perfectly entitled to open mail addressed to the board. Besides, Marcus Steevens *was* her boarder and all of his things *were* gone. She begrudgingly admitted that the teacher had suggested his intentions of leaving a few weeks earlier, but she hadn't taken him seriously. And he certainly had *not* given her adequate formal notice in writing.

"And the second thing," Jonah's dad said, finally interrupting Betty's personal musings on lost rent money, "is that Charlotte Barkhouse has apparently run away."

Ruth snorted. "Not related, my rear end! The Mounties have been knocking on every door since nine o'clock this morning asking if anyone's ever seen the two of them cavorting together."

Nine o'clock.

His mother had received a phone call from Ruth at nine that very morning. She'd known then that something was up and that's why she'd shooed him and Beaz away.

They'd spent the whole day on Oak Island oblivious to the biggest news to hit Western Shore since last winter, when a slightly drunk Stan MacDonald had driven his new Chevy onto the frozen salt water—the vehicle cracked through the ice and the truck was towed away for good. Ruth did all the driving now in their old Pontiac and Stan's mishap was one story she never repeated at church socials.

"So has anyone ever seen them together?" Jonah's dad asked.

The room fell silent.

Jonah, peering in from the coat room, held his breath. Somebody must have seen them. Surely he wasn't the only one who knew, was he?

The door of the schoolhouse creaked open, letting in another straggler to the meeting.

Marshall Delray.

The note!

Jonah was off the hook. Someone else knew too. He didn't have to say what he'd seen, tell what he'd heard. Marshall would do it.

All eyes turned to the back of the room.

"What about you, Marshall?" Betty asked. "Have you ever seen your teacher and Charlotte fraternizing?"

No!!! Jonah thought desperately. *The word is too big...*

Marshall scratched his head. "Huh?"

Betty sighed. "Courtin'."

A vein pulsed on Marshall's jaw.

Tell them! Jonah pleaded silently.

Marshall rubbed at the grease smeared on his hands. "Nope. Never." Then he turned to Jonah. "What about you, kid? Know anything?"

In the background, Jonah heard another one of those darned bees buzzing—Western Shore must be the bee capital of Nova Scotia.

If someone had asked Jonah why he dreaded telling

what he saw, he wouldn't have had an answer. It could've had something to do with the daggers in Marshall's eyes, wordlessly warning him to keep his trap shut about the note.

Or it might have been the memory of Charlotte's bedraggled clothing when she'd left the schoolhouse— and how Jonah suspected he knew what it all meant but he wasn't ready to give it life yet.

Regardless, he had to say something. "I saw Charlotte in Mr. Steevens' car yesterday after school. I thought he was giving her a ride home."

"I knew it!" Ruth snapped.

There was a collective sigh around the room signalling that the meeting was adjourned and that mothers didn't need to lock up their daughters from a deranged maniac running loose in the community.

"You'll have to tell the Mounties," Jonah's dad said, resting his hand on his son's shoulder. "Charlotte's family will want to know."

"Young men in love," his mother sighed. "If he'd only waited a year or two more no one would have batted an eye."

Sidling up beside them, Ruth MacDonald said, "That's what you get for hiring a foreigner *and* a new graduate. I always said that a *single* twenty-one-year-old male teacher would be trouble."

"Twenty-one minus sixteen. Five years. That's the same age difference as you and Stan, isn't it?" Jonah's mom said.

"It's not the same thing, Muriel! I was already twenty-two and my husband was twenty-seven."

"Yes, you were. Charlotte is only sixteen and not old enough to know any better."

Ruth glared.

As he walked toward his bike, Jonah reviewed his mother's words. Maybe, just maybe, his mother had managed one more time to best her least favourite neighbour.

Way to go again, Mom!

"Hey!"

Jonah spun around. Marshall, with his arms folded, stood like an oak tree in front of the rosebush.

"Yeah?" Jonah said.

"Did you deliver my note?"

"Yeah."

"Did you tell him it was from me?"

"No."

Marshall squinted, tugging the gold chain around his neck. "Did you read it?"

Swallowing, Jonah opened his mouth—

"We have to go, son," his dad called.

"Sure, Dad!" And turning back toward Marshall, he mouthed the word no.

Was it still a lie when you didn't say the word out loud?

Sam Cooke ambled down the stairs, his rubber boots swashing and squishing down each step. As usual, the Wharf Prophet was whistling. This time it was a new hit by Elvis Presley—"Heartbreak Hotel."

CHAPTER 7

DEACON DELRAY SPENT MOST NIGHTS RUNNING up a tab at the Dine and Dance and his days patrolling as an RCMP officer. Jonah's mom often said she'd never seen a person more poorly named than Deacon—he was the farthest thing from a church-going man there ever was. But he knew how to keep his stretch of highway along the South Shore safe. That was something no one disputed.

He was also Marshall's older brother.

Jonah stared at the buttons on Constable Delray's uniform while he answered the officer's questions.

No, he didn't think they were leaving for good when he saw them in the car.

No, he didn't know about the disappearance until the meeting.

No, he didn't suspect that Charlotte was running away.

Those were his answers.

Keeping his fingers crossed behind his back, Jonah feverishly prayed in his head. *Don't ask what I heard them say…don't ask where I was all day today…don't ask about Charlotte's clothes…*

"What was Charlotte wearing?"

Breathing in and slowly puffing the air back through his lips, Jonah thought.

And thought.

"Was it the same thing she had on in school?" his mother prodded, adding, "You know, Deacon, teenage boys don't pay attention to other people's wardrobes."

"I'm pretty sure it was the same clothes," Jonah answered. He almost added that he didn't notice anything different, but that would have been a lie. And he was terrified of telling a lie ever since hearing Reverend Shupe's fiery sermon on hell.

"What about you, Beasley?" the constable asked. "Did you notice anything unusual?"

Beaz cringed. Jonah knew it was at the sound of his full name—it would have been even worse if the constable had said "Beasley Humphrey." That was his name, Beasley Humphrey Hodder. Only Beaz's mother hauled out the Humphrey, when Beaz was in a manure pile of trouble. Jonah wondered if hearing the names rhymed off over the airwaves of Western Shore hurt more than the strap his friend was destined to get by the time he raced home.

Probably not.

"He called her 'dear' in school yesterday," Beaz answered, rubbing at some island dirt still coating his hand.

"Anything else?" Constable Delray asked.

"Nope."

"Well, I guess that's it, then," Abraham Morgan said in his "lawyer" voice. He stood to indicate the interview was over.

Constable Delray took the hint and stood up as well. "If you two think of something more, let me know."

"You boys must be starved," Jonah's mom said. "Beaz, why don't you phone your dad and invite him to join us for supper. We've got enough ham to feed a small army."

Jonah suspected his mom knew more about the workings of Beaz's family than she let on. Never once had she invited the family for supper. But now that Mrs. Hodder was away—

The phone call was made and soon Mr. Hodder arrived on the doorstep with a friendly grin. "Thanks so much, Muriel and Abraham. Couldn't quite stomach my scrambled eggs one more time."

The Hodders had a chicken coop and Beaz often complained about eating eggs for breakfast, dinner, and supper on days when his mother couldn't sell all of their eggs. "You weren't at the town meeting, were you?" Jonah's father asked Daniel Hodder.

Mr. Hodder shook his head. "Just got in from Bridgewater when Beaz telephoned me for supper. What's the uproar about this time?"

Jonah's dad paused. "Well, the boys here already heard most of the details…in fact, they knew more than the rest of us."

Beaz belched. "'Scuse me."

Mr. Hodder frowned. "Are you in trouble, Beaz?"

"Nothing like that," Jonah's father assured him. "It's a somewhat delicate subject, and I wouldn't normally mention it in front of the boys, but they did have some information to pass along to Constable Delray."

Jonah held his breath. Everything seemed so serious. He felt a twinge of guilt at leaving out some of the details… but they weren't important…were they?

"Charlotte Barkhouse ran off with the teacher," his mom said bluntly.

"Ah," Daniel Hodder said, looking relieved.

Maybe he thought Beaz was into some mischief that Mrs. Hodder would hear about, Jonah thought.

"Betty's 'shocked' and 'outraged,'" Abraham chuckled.

"No doubt," Mr. Hodder said as a grin spread across his face too.

"No skeletons in her closet, I'm sure," Jonah's mom said.

Mr. Hodder sobered. "Will the police go after them?"

"That's up to Charlotte's parents." Jonah's dad sighed. "They may let it go…Marcus Steevens is barely twenty-one."

"Sometimes scandal dies down faster that way," Mr. Hodder said.

Jonah liked it better when he eavesdropped from the pantry. Being included in the adults' conversation made him feel responsible. He pushed the bits of ham and mashed potatoes around on his plate, his appetite gone. "May Beaz and I be excused?"

"Of course, honey," his mother said, winking. "You boys grab some cookies and run off while I put the kettle on."

"Tide's in," Beaz said. "Wanna do a little fishing?"

"Sure," Jonah said, hoping that just this once, they wouldn't bump into Sam Cooke—the whistling Wharf Prophet could really creep a person out.

Soon they were settled on the end of the wharf, listening to the splash of the waves against the wood beams underneath the planks.

"My mother can be nice, you know," Beaz said out of the blue.

"Okay," Jonah said.

"I mean it. She has a lot on her mind, is all. Like my grandmother and uncle—"

"I know about your grandmother being sick," Jonah replied. "But what's wrong with your uncle?"

Beaz kicked his foot against the wood and shrugged. "Not sure. He's always moving to a new town and asking for money. Every time she gets a letter from Uncle Craig it's like a thundercloud appears over her head."

"Is that why she sells eggs and bread?" Jonah had often wondered why Beaz's mother worked so hard to make money. It didn't seem like the family needed it. Mr. Hodder was a carpenter with clients all the way from New Germany to the South End of Halifax. The Hodder house was a snug two-storey that always looked freshly painted and well kept.

"Partly," Beaz replied. "Dad told me once that Mom had a hard life growing up. She likes to have extra money, 'just in case.'"

"Hmm." It was all he could think to say at first. Then he added, "Beaz."

"What?"

"I heard Mr. Steevens and Charlotte talking when I went back for my lunch pail yesterday. I hid behind the curtain and watched them leave. I think they were kissing, or something."

"Or something?"

Casting his rod out again, it was Jonah's turn to shrug.

"Hmm," Beaz said.

Quietly they stared out as the orange rays from the sunset spilled over them.

"Beaz!"

"What?"

"Look!" Jonah grabbed Beaz's arm and pointed to the tiny piece of Oak Island visible from the wharf. "Smoke!"

An island of secrets, both past and present. Jonah knew he needed to investigate—starting with his brother.

CHAPTER 8

Caleb's room played an uncomfortable role in the Morgan home—somewhere between an awkward spare bedroom and a ghostly collection of memories. Never a shrine, though; Jonah's mother had seen to that.

"This quilt's seen its last washing," she said one day about a month ago, pulling the covering off the twin bed and tossing it in with her rag pile.

She'd walked past her husband, Abraham, in the hallway and Jonah had quietly observed from the door of his own bedroom.

"Don't," his mother had said, holding up her hand to his father before he even spoke a word. "I've made up my mind. Your mother sleeps there when she visits. I'll not have my mother-in-law saying I don't keep the house up to the Morgan standards."

She didn't say it, Jonah thought. But he suspected that her annoyance reflected a sad understanding that somehow life had to move forward even when she secretly hoped it might not.

Stepping into Caleb's room on this breezy early summer evening, Jonah breathed deeply. He was looking for something, a clue to how and when his brother's name had been etched into the timbers of the Money Pit.

The window stood open, welcoming the sunset and fresh air—this wasn't the stifled room of a tragically lost sixteen-year-old. Jonah had been twelve at the time of the accident and even though everyone from Ruth MacDonald to Grandma Morgan had hugged him and whispered, "So sorry for your loss," Jonah hadn't shed one tear.

Truth was, he didn't *feel* a loss. Of course he noticed his brother's empty chair at the dinner table and the sad glances between his parents from time to time, but there was no hole left in Jonah's daily life.

He missed Caleb's occasional slap on the shoulder, but Beaz was more like Jonah's brother—not his twin, though. Even though they were born on the same day, Beaz wasn't opposed to bending the truth if necessary. Plus they looked nothing alike. Jonah was a whole head taller than Beaz and Jonah's blond hair hung straight as straw while Beaz's thick brown curls resembled tightly wound steel wool.

Sifting through the collection of notebooks and drawings in Caleb's bottom drawer, Jonah wondered if it should worry him that he didn't mourn his brother.

He supposed he could say that he'd loved Caleb but had never felt close to him. In spite of his solemn thoughts, he smiled. Ruth MacDonald would be scandalized. No one should admit to not missing a brother.

Jonah's chest tightened as he reached for the last remaining Hilroy scribbler in the drawer. He blew away the dust and stared. In the subject line, Caleb had written, Oak Island Diary, 1956.

So Oak Island really isn't all mine. Shaking his head slightly, Jonah tried to dismiss the selfish thought. His parents had never made him feel like he was in competition with Caleb—that was something that had been sprouting wickedly on its own after he'd heard his brother's eulogy.

Rev. Shupe's words echoed even now…*Caleb was a fine young man worthy of admiration. He was a top scholar and athlete and was known for his ingenuity…*

Ever since those words had been uttered, Jonah wondered what he would be known for…fishing off the government wharf? Not much of a legacy.

He flipped open Caleb's notebook.

July 1st, 1956
Happy 89th birthday Canada!
Ben and I are going back to the Island tomorrow. It's our first trip over this summer. Last year we went down in the shaft about 20 feet. We're just exploring,

really. The shaft is flooded and there's nothing the two of us can do about it. I guess we're holding out hope that we'll find a few gold coins. Rumours are whispered that every once in a while someone "salts" the mine to fool future treasure hunters. I wouldn't mind finding a bit of that salt. Ha!

Ben.

Jonah had forgotten about him. Ben had been Caleb's equivalent of Beaz. They'd been best friends from the time they were in diapers until Ben moved away not long before Caleb's accident.

July 9th, 1956

The summer is over almost before it's started! Ben is moving next week. His father got a job in Alberta on the oil fields and they're leaving right away. They aren't even taking time to sell the house first. Just when we are finally getting somewhere with our treasure hunting. This is rotten!

Jonah flicked the page to see two more entries.

July 27th, 1956

Marshall said he'd go with me to Oak Island next time. He's not the sharpest knife in the drawer when it comes to school, but he's been helping me rebuild the engine on the Buick. Dad said once I have it running, it's mine!

The humid air in the room grew close. He never knew that Caleb and Marshall had spent any time together. Marshall was only a year younger than Caleb had been, but they had been four years apart in school thanks to Marshall flunking two grades and Caleb skipping one.

The next entry was the final one:

August 3rd, 1956

This isn't turning into much of a diary about Oak Island. Marshall and I went back to search for the other tunnels rumoured to be scattered over the island. We found a stone with markings near Smith's Cove. Maybe the Money Pit is a Decoy? I read Penn Leary's theory on the treasure. He thinks the treasure is the original writings of Sir Francis Bacon—the rumoured author of Shakespeare's plays. A bunch of parchments don't sound like much of a treasure even if I do like Shakespeare. I think I'll spend the rest of the summer working on the Buick. Charlotte wants to be the first to take a ride.

Charlotte.
Marshall.
Oak Island.

The names connected Jonah to his brother more than his own scattered memories. He and Caleb had been apart in age, but now their lives were intertwined in the social fabric and folklore of Western Shore.

His eyes stung with tears.

CHAPTER 9

JONAH HELPED BEAZ COLLECT EGGS FIRST THING Saturday morning. The warm, stuffy shed smelled like— well, a chicken coop. That's why Jonah had only one hand free to dig through the straw. His nose was pinched with the other.

"You'll get used to it," Beaz said. He scooped up two eggs at once and gently placed them in the wire basket.

Jonah tried not to think about it. The smell. And how chicken-coop germs were still being sucked in through his mouth. Sunlight streamed through a narrow window illuminating dancing chicken dust. "Sure," Jonah said in a squeaky, nasally voice. He'd already finished his own chores and collecting eggs was the last thing on Beaz's list.

"I didn't sleep last night. I was thinking about that smoke."

"Me too," Jonah said. He'd been thinking more about Caleb than the fire, but both roads led to Oak Island. "Dad said there's no one living over there now."

"You asked him?" Beaz yelped. The eggs jostled in the mesh basket.

"Not a chance! He started talking about the Barkhouses at breakfast."

"Charlotte's family? Why? Did you tell him what you saw at the schoolhouse?"

"No! Dad just started rambling about her family. They have one of those cabins that used to be on Oak Island. They attached it to the back of their house as a third bedroom around the time Charlotte was born. Lots of people in Western Shore have Oak Island cabin additions."

"Sounds drafty," Beaz said.

"Anyway, Dad said no one lives on the island now."

"Maybe there's a hobo."

"Yeah," Jonah said. "A hobo hops off a train and says, 'Maybe I should take a swim over to that there island.'"

"Not a hobo, then. A hermit."

Jonah cleared his throat and recited, "There's a story I'm told, of a man that is old, who lives on the Isle of Oaks…"

"Quit it," Beaz said. "With your nose plugged like that, you sound like Ruth MacDonald singing in the Christmas pageant."

Outside the coop, Jonah inhaled the fresh air. "So are we going to the island today, or what?"

Beaz turned pea soup green. "Don't know. So far we've seen a dead rabbit and now mysterious smoke. Maybe someone's trying to tell us something."

"Son?"

Beaz spun around. "Yes, sir."

"The Captain wants two dozen eggs delivered this morning. Run them by before you two disappear to heaven knows where."

"Two dozen? Again?"

Beaz's dad smiled. "Church potluck tomorrow. He's making devilled eggs."

Who's the Captain? Jonah wondered.

"Sure, Dad." Beaz counted the eggs out and put them into a paper sack. "Dad built some cabinets on Sam Cooke's boat last summer," Beaz explained. "Ever since, he calls him the Captain."

It was a weird thing, how friends could read each other's minds—most of the time, anyway. Beaz didn't know how Sam Cooke's ominous words just one week ago had made the blood chill in Jonah's veins—and had made him think twice about exploring Oak Island. "I call him the 'Wharf Prophet,'" Jonah said.

"Since when?"

"I don't know. He predicts all kinds of stuff. Isn't that what a prophet is supposed to do? Foresee the future?"

"You tell me," Beaz said. "You're the one who goes to church all the time. Didn't prophets live back in the pyramid days?"

Several minutes later, the two boys had reached the top of Sam Cooke's secluded driveway. Jonah stared. He'd never been up to the Wharf Prophet's house before. It tilted crookedly to one side and looked like it might slip off the hill and into the ocean if the wind caught it just right. "Creepy," he said, squinting. Maybe if he blinked again, the weathered grey clapboards would cinch together and straighten up.

Setting the eggs down on the sloping doorstep, Beaz knocked.

They waited.

"Hello!" Beaz shouted, knocking again. "Mr. Cooke?"

A few more moments passed.

"Do you hear that?" Jonah whispered.

The whistling drifted from behind the house…the mournful melody of "My Bonnie Lies Over the Ocean."

"MR. COOKE!"

A creaky hinge squeaked in the distance and a door slammed. "Who's there?"

"Beaz, with your eggs."

"I was in the barn," the old fisherman said as he rounded the side of the house.

Jonah gasped. Sam Cooke's silver hair stuck out wildly in a million directions. *He looks like a mad scientist…*

"Two dozen?" Sam Cooke asked.

"Yes, sir."

The Wharf Prophet cleaned his hands with a scrap of torn gingham. "I'll go get your money."

Jonah jabbed Beaz as the old fisherman disappeared inside his house. "Did you see that?"

"What?"

"He was crying."

"He was not!"

"Yes he was. His eyes were all watery and his hair looked like he'd just flown a prop plane over Antarctica."

"It was a bit out of control," Beaz admitted.

"And his hands," Jonah said. "He was wiping off blood."

The door of the crooked house creaked back open and the wild-haired Wharf Prophet jangled coins in his stained hands.

Beaz held his palm open and his face crinkled up like he'd just seen a ghost. "Thank…thank…th…thank you, sir." He reached into his pocket to fish out some pennies.

Sam Cooke waved his arm and the red on his fingers danced in the morning light. "Keep the change," he said. "Now scat! I'm busy."

Beaz stumbled down the beach gravel driveway.

Out of breath, Jonah caught up with him around the bend. "Wait up!"

"I've delivered eggs here a gazillion times," Beaz whispered. "The Capt…Mr. Cooke has *always* been in a good mood…normal."

"Not today." Jonah pointed out the obvious. "As a matter of fact I think he's been in a dither for about a week now."

"What do you mean?"

Jonah wished he'd kept his big mouth shut. If he told Beaz about the "prophecy," his friend would be scared witless. Mix that up with the smoke, the dead rabbit, the teacher running off with Charlotte, and Marshall Delray...

Dang! He hadn't told Beaz about Marshall's note, either.

"Forget about it," Jonah said. "Let's just get out of here and go to the island."

"What about the smoke?"

Shrugging, Jonah sighed. "Can't be much to it, or the community would be in an uproar over that, too."

And that was that. Problem solved.

The way Jonah figured it, in the last two days the quiet community of Western Shore had turned upside down and sideways with Charlotte's disappearance. What was done was done and Jonah still had his heart set on finding Captain Kidd's treasure. As long as Beaz's mother was tucked away in Halifax, and Marshall Delray was pumping gas in Chester, he felt like the coast was clear.

There was no way a little smoke was going to mess up a perfect summer. He was going to do the one thing Caleb hadn't—uncover the secrets buried at Oak Island.

CHAPTER 10

JONAH FELT THE BREEZE ON HIS CHEEK BEFORE hearing the leaves rustle on the trees. Today, the island seemed less ghostly. After all, ghosts didn't light fires. Living, breathing human beings did that, and for some reason the thought of other trespassers on the island didn't seem as frightening as it had the day before.

He wasn't sure why. Perhaps it was because he'd faced Marshall *and* Deacon Delray last night and had held his own. Or maybe it was because Beaz's mother had called long distance even later last night to inform Beaz's dad that she'd be away at least another two weeks. Or maybe it was because this morning the wild-looking Wharf Prophet had seemed to lose some of his truth-telling credibility by resembling an escapee from the insane asylum.

"Let's go straight to the pit," Jonah said. "No one bothered us there yesterday. We won't even go near the end of the island where we saw the smoke."

"Yeah," Beaz nodded. "If we don't bother them, they won't bother us." He unloaded the rope and shovels while

Jonah tied the *Gingerale* to a hefty piece of driftwood. "What about the rabbit?" he asked.

"Brought this," Jonah said, holding up a clothespin. "For the smell."

Soon they had their supplies in a haphazard pile near the shafts: yards of rope, two flashlights, picks and shovels, mounds of food, two mason jars filled with drinking water, and burlap bags—just in case they hit pay dirt.

The rabbit was gone.

"What do you think happened to it?"

Jonah shrugged. "Don't know. A wild animal dragged it away or dropped it in the pit?" Beaming a light down into the shaft, he leaned forward. "Goes down a long ways," he observed.

"You wanna go in first?" Beaz asked.

"Sure." Jonah tried not to think about dead rabbits, wild animals, or smoking fires as he tied one end of the rope around his waist and pulled the knot snug. "What can we anchor to?"

Beaz pointed to the remains of a thick spruce. "Wind it around that."

After securing the rope to the stump, Jonah shone his light down into the pit again. He didn't see much. The shaft seemed a long way down when he thought about hanging by a thread. "Let the rope out slowly," he said, gripping the beams like giant rungs on a ladder.

"Sure thing," Beaz answered.

Digging his shoes into the dark soil, Jonah descended into the Money Pit. He gripped his flashlight under his armpit and that made holding on awkward. The shadows grew darker and he could feel his heart hammering in his chest. "Just a sec, Beaz. Wind some back up. That's too much!"

Beaz hauled back the slack and the rope stretched taut. "Better?"

"Better! I'll poke around here for a minute." Jonah shone the flashlight around the musty pit—the dampness weighted the air. He stared into the sunny opening above him and calculated that he was about fifteen feet down. "Hey there, little fella," he said as he noticed a dangling earthworm clinging to the damp soil. Fortunately there were no decomposing rabbits.

Suddenly, the earthworm lost its battle with gravity and plummeted into the darkness.

"Beaz?" Jonah shouted.

"Yup?"

"Just checking you're still there." Brushing some dirt off a splintered beam, Jonah grabbed at the wood and shimmied himself up onto it. He balanced precariously, concerned that if he wasn't careful he'd soon take a swan dive after the worm. He didn't even have time to catch his breath before the beam shifted, loosening more dirt from the shaft and pelting soil down on his face. Gripping the rope, he noticed that his hands were slick with sweat and icy chills sparked up his back. Maybe somewhere at the bottom of the shaft was a great slithering mass of earthworms and rotting rabbits—a cushioned layer of protection for crazy treasure hunters who lost their grip and careened below.

He gagged and then heaved a sigh of relief that Beaz wasn't there to witness how he was wimping out. Inside the Money Pit everything felt not real and too real at the same time. Suddenly Oak Island treasure hunting seemed like a shirt he'd tried on that was three sizes too big. Caleb's shirt.

That was until he flicked his light around again and this time it reflected off something shiny on the wooden beam beside him. He reached out—

"Beaz? Beaz!" he yelped, barely breathing. "Haul me up. Now!"

"Hang on a sec," Beaz's voice echoed back. "I don't eat as many cookies as you."

Beaz wasn't kidding. He *was* a tad on the scrawny side compared to Jonah's broadening shoulders.

Looking for a secure place to stash the newly discovered treasure while he clambered his way out, Jonah settled on sticking it into his mouth and now sucked in air through his nostrils. Then he tucked the flashlight inside his shirt pocket. Right now he needed the muscles of both his arms more than the power of speech or a flashlight. Dirt crumbled underneath his feet as he scrambled to reach the top.

Don't swallow, he reminded himself.

Red-faced and taking deep breaths by the time Jonah reached the surface, Beaz grumbled, "What's the hurry? Where's the fire?"

Jonah spit into his hand and displayed his prize.

"What? How? Where?"

"A heart-shaped locket," Jonah said. "Sitting in plain sight on a beam. Must have come loose when a bunch of the dirt fell."

"Holy hillbilly!" Beaz leapt up onto the spruce stump and danced an elfish-looking jig. "You know what this means, dontcha?"

"Yep." Jonah carefully dried the spit-covered locket on his pant leg. "We struck gold."

CHAPTER 11

THE BOTTOM OF THE *GINGERALE* SCRAPED against the rocks as Jonah launched it into the water. Day two of Oak Island exploration had ended early. Beaz had taken a quick trip into the Money Pit after Jonah had climbed out, but turned up zip. Still, they were ecstatic that Jonah had struck gold!

Now they were packed up and on the way back to the mainland. And suddenly Jonah realized he'd never actually given much thought to what they'd do if they found treasure. Who would they tell? How would they escape a scolding for sneaking onto the island in the first place?

If they'd found the whole kit and caboodle, millions in pirate's gold, maybe all would be forgiven.

But a single heart-shaped locket without a chain? Was that worth endangering Beaz's hide for?

"It must be really old," Beaz said.

"Yeah, it needs a good cleaning." The locket was

wrapped in a rag and jammed into Jonah's pants pocket—he couldn't risk pirate's treasure falling overboard while they were rowing back to shore.

Moving against the tide always made for extra work, but this time their muscles were fuelled with adrenalin from their discovery. They were out past the tip of the island when Jonah felt the cold seeping into his shoes.

Water!

"Row faster, Beaz."

"What's the hurry?"

"We're sinking."

"Dang! Someone's gotta bail…and we need to plug the hole…and, dang!"

"You bail. I'll keep rowing," Jonah said. He grabbed both oars and battled alone against the tide.

Beaz crawled along the bottom of the boat, sloshing through the water. "Where's a bucket? Where's your lunchbox?"

"Under the rope. Hurry, Beaz!"

"I am!"

"Plug the hole."

Beaz scooped. "I can't!"

The *Gingerale* slumped low in the water. No matter how hard he tried, Jonah couldn't get the rowboat to draw closer to the mainland. "Dump the cargo!"

Over the sides of the boat, they threw shovels, rope,

and anything else that wasn't attached. Jonah grabbed a Mason jar and helped Beaz bail.

"We're gonna lose her," Beaz shouted after a few minutes. "We have to swim for it."

Jonah tore his shirt over his head. "Just wear your trunks!"

Beaz stared, turning pale as the boat gushed water. "We can't. How will I explain what happened to my clothes?"

"We'll figure that out later."

"It's a long way to the mainland."

Shaking his head, Jonah said, "We're closer to the northwest tip of the island. Go there!"

"Wait! What about the locket?" Beaz said, suddenly sitting very still as if frozen solid. The water was slapping against the benches now.

The icy cold of Mahone Bay had numbed Jonah up to his knees. How could he have forgotten? Maybe his brain was frozen too. Grabbing the pants floating beside him, he whipped the handkerchief from the pocket.

Now what?

He wished his swimming trunks had a pocket, a secret compartment, anything, to keep the locket from sinking to the bottom of the bay. But he had nothing and neither did Beaz.

"Hurry!" Beaz yelled. "Think of something."

Just like in the Money Pit, Jonah knew he needed both

of his arms free. Only this time instead of climbing, he'd be swimming in the chilly waters of Mahone Bay. He unwrapped the cloth from around the locket and stuck the nickel-sized piece of jewellery back into his mouth. It still tasted like cold dirt and tin.

"Don't swallow it!" Beaz yelled, diving overboard.

Easy for you to say, Jonah thought, splashing into the waves.

Cold.

Too cold.

He forced his arms and legs to move—they cooperated.

His pants floated along beside him for the first few strokes until they became waterlogged. Then, with barely a final whimper, the *Gingerale* was sucked under the surface as well.

Jonah wiggled the locket under his tongue and clenched his teeth together to make a protective dam to filter air. Now he could breathe through both his mouth and nose as he skimmed through the waves.

The current latched onto him and he struggled harder. At least the tide was on their side now, as it drew them back toward Oak Island. Beaz reached the shore first and waved to Jonah.

Flipping onto his back and kicking with his feet, Jonah tried to rest and inhale more deeply. Maybe he'd be better off with the locket clenched in his fist than with it blocking his airflow—but he didn't want to chance it. After a moment, he turned back over and caught sight of Beaz wildly waving and jumping from the shallow water.

What's his problem? Jonah thought. Why was Beaz acting so crazy?

"Bee have…," Beaz shouted.

Bee what? Beehive?

Jonah lifted his head and waved back. He opened his lips to say something but changed his mind. The locket might fall out. Besides, Beaz would never hear him muttering through clenched teeth from this far away.

SMACK!

A wave pounded Jonah in the back of his head and he slid under the water just as he was filtering in a big gulp of air through his teeth. Salt water stung the back of his throat and he gagged and coughed as he pushed his way back to the surface. He spit out the bitter water and forced himself to gulp steady measures of air.

Kick, stroke, kick, stroke… it felt like an eternity.

"Take my hand," Beaz shouted finally.

Jonah bobbed his head out of the water. Beaz had swum out to him. Grabbing on to his friend's outstretched hand, Jonah kicked his feet. After a quick moment, they were close enough to shore to stand on the ocean's rocky floor.

"I tried to tell you," Beaz said, the water still up to his shoulders. "Big wave."

Jonah spit again and snorted the salt water out of his nose. "Thought you said beehive." Chilled and nauseous, he sloshed out of the water and collapsed onto the shore. "That was lucky."

"Yeah, but now we're stuck here." Beaz lowered his voice to a whisper. "And I think we're near where we saw the smoke last night."

Maybe not so lucky?

"We'll figure some way to get home. We can build a raft or something."

"We'll have to wait until the tide changes before trying to swim home," Beaz said. "It'll be easier then."

Jonah licked his lips, wishing he could have a swig of the lukewarm water from the Mason jar.

"Where is it?" Beaz asked.

"The bottom of the ocean with the *Gingerale* and my pants," Jonah answered, wondering how Beaz could always read his mind. "I used the jar to help bail, remember?"

Beaz frowned. "I think the salt water pickled your brain."

"What?"

"I was asking you about the locket."

A nasty brew was concocting in Jonah's stomach, salt water swishing and swirling, making him feel like he'd eaten some sun-ripened devilled eggs. "I don't…"

"You lost it?"

Jonah thought back to the last time he remembered the locket in his mouth—right before the wave pummelled him. His teeth started to chatter and he rubbed his arms to get warm. "I think…I swallowed the water…"

"And the locket fell out?"

He remembered gagging as the salt water hit the back of his throat. "I think my parents should have named me George, Sam, or Frank…something that isn't cursed already."

"What are you talking about? I think you've got a fever."

"Jonah. My name. You know, the Bible guy who ended up shipwrecked and got swallowed by a whale."

Beaz rolled his eyes. "You're delirious."

"Nope, but I feel like I'm gonna barf."

Shivering, Beaz stepped back. "Just in case there's projectile vomiting," he explained.

"I think it would be a good thing if there was," Jonah said. "Because I'm pretty sure I swallowed the locket."

CHAPTER 12

"Lucky it's hot as blazes," Beaz said a few minutes later. Salt water dripped from his hair onto his shoulders and goosebumps peppered his bare arms.

"That's one thing going our way." Jonah stared at the waves. His eyes were glued to the spot where the *Gingerale* had sunk. "Dang rocks."

"What if we don't make it back by supper?" Beaz's face went from purplish-blue to white.

"We will," Jonah said. He hoped he sounded more convinced than he really was. Too bad the tide had been headed in the opposite direction when they'd jumped ship. "Wish we had life jackets."

"But we both swim great!"

Jonah knew Beaz's mother had thrown him off the wharf during high tide into twenty feet of water when he was just seven. Beaz often told the story as if it was a hilarious way to learn to swim. Jonah, who'd experienced a more gentle approach—swimming lessons at Lake Mush-A-Mush—thought it was just another bizarre chapter in Beaz's see-saw life.

"We couldn't take the chance with the currents and the tide," Jonah said. "Even when the tide turns we need *something* to hang on to."

"Sounds like a *freeze our behind off* problem," Beaz muttered.

"Maybe there's an old boat or raft. Let's look around a bit."

Beaz grabbed his arm. "What about the hermit…or, whoever it was that had a campfire?"

Be sure your sins will find you out. The saying echoed in Jonah's brain. They weren't supposed to be on Oak Island, but they'd come anyway. Now the *Gingerale* lay at the bottom of the ocean and the locket was sliding around in Jonah's innards. What if their misdeeds were discovered by another mysterious island trespasser—or worse, what if their parents found out where they had been? Then what?

"Just keep quiet," Jonah whispered. "Besides, if there *is* someone here they might have a boat we can use."

"We're gonna steal a boat?" Beaz's eyes widened.

It didn't sit right with Jonah either. If lying sent you straight to hell, then stealing a boat likely landed you in the extra-crispy section. "No." He sighed. "And what in the world am I gonna do about that locket?"

"Sounds like a *poop your behind off* problem." Beaz held his stomach as he laughed.

"Not funny."

"You're gonna have to check. Every time you go."

"But what if it gets stuck inside? How fast does stuff go through you, anyway?"

"Don't know," Beaz said. "Mr. Steevens didn't teach us that."

"Yeah," Jonah said. "He was obviously too busy mooning over Charlotte." The queasy feeling came back in his stomach. He wasn't sure if it was because of the locket rolling around his intestines or remembering what he'd witnessed at the schoolhouse only two days earlier.

The boys stumbled over the rocky shoreline, combing for driftwood and rope—searching for "treasure" of a different kind that could be used to lash logs together and build a raft.

"There's nothing here," Beaz said finally. "I never should have let you talk me into coming over to this stupid island."

"Me? You've been yapping about it since Mr. Steevens made us do that project on pirates." Jonah's pulse hammered in his ears.

Beaz squatted on a rock and pulled his knees up to his chin. "I'm gonna get killed when my mother hears about this."

"We'll figure something out," Jonah said, knowing their squabbles were always over before they really got started. Besides, they only had a few hours before the tide changed—that's when the distance would be the shortest to swim and the current would help propel them home.

Hopefully in time for supper.

"Let's look inland," Jonah said finally. He climbed up the rocks and headed for the trees.

"Wait for me!" Beaz hissed in a loud whisper.

A narrow path dipped into the forest. It wasn't worn down to the dirt, just trampled grass looking like it had recently been walked on.

"I don't like this," Beaz said.

"We've got no choice."

The sun filtered through the trees and it seemed as if even the birds held their breath—every living thing was silent.

A twig snapped and a voice boomed, "Well, look at what the sea dragged in!"

Jonah jumped and spun around. The blood drained from his head and his ears started ringing. Was he fainting?

Beaz yelped and covered his face.

The stranger's voice seemed oddly familiar to Jonah but he couldn't match it to the curly hair and pale youthful face speckled with sparse whiskers. Who was the bum sloppily dressed in a plaid shirt and denim pants?

"What's the matter? You two look like you've seen a ghost."

Shutting his eyes hard, Jonah jiggled his head. He forced his eyes back open and now understood what his brain was screaming. "Mr. Steevens," he choked.

"The smoke last night," Beaz said, lowering his hands. "It was you?"

"You caught me red-handed," Mr. Steevens chuckled. "Thought I'd hang out here for a bit. Do some...thinking before heading back to Ontario. Apparently my little campfire wasn't such a bright idea if I didn't want anyone to know I was here."

Jonah gawked past Mr. Steevens' shoulder. He couldn't help it. Charlotte must be here too. Would she stroll out of their Oak Island love nest looking just as wildly out of place as his former teacher? What would *she* be wearing?

"You look different."

"You always have a way of stating the obvious, Beaz. Guess you're used to seeing me stuffed into a suit and tie."

"Guess so," Jonah agreed. He'd never given it much thought before. Mr. Steevens had been a teacher—not a person. Dressed in jeans instead of a suit, he looked like a big goof who could be pumpin' gas alongside Marshall Delray.

"So why are you two here, washed up like some scrawny driftwood?"

Jonah turned around and gave Beaz a look. One that

said, *Zip it and let me do the talking.* "We were on our boat in the bay and it sprung a leak."

Beaz raised his eyebrows.

Jonah's shoulders relaxed as he quickly reviewed his words. *Nope, no lie there.*

"So you need a ride back."

"Yup."

Scratching at his stubble, Mr. Steevens said, "I didn't really want anyone to know I was here."

"Sounds good to us," Jonah said. "We don't want anyone to know we were out in the boat."

The teacher frowned.

"You know parents." Beaz chuckled artificially. "They'd…worry. You can drop us off over there." He pointed to the end of Crandall's Point Road.

Now Jonah raised his eyebrows. Beaz should've kept it zipped. Now they'd have to walk twice as far—in swimming trunks, with no shoes!

"You two promise you'll keep quiet?" Mr. Steevens glanced behind him. "I need to…time to think."

Feeling as if he'd been sucked into something murky again—something that kept following him around like a bad penny, Jonah wondered what the teacher would say if he knew how many secrets he'd already buried. "It's no skin off our nose. You keep our secret, we'll keep yours."

"Fine with me, then. Let's go."

They helped Mr. Steevens drag his skiff out of the bushes. Just as they were about to launch the boat, Beaz shouted, "Look at that!"

Scattered along the shore of Oak Island were three shoes and two shirts—the current had reunited them with bits of their clothing.

"Both of my shoes," Beaz yelped. "And my shirt!"

Jonah smiled. Beaz's hide would stay intact now that he wouldn't have to explain his missing shoes to his mother when she returned home. He gathered his own shirt and single shoe. It would take some manoeuvring but he'd figure out a way to explain his missing clothing.

All without telling a lie.

His smile faded as he watched Mr. Steevens dip the oars into the surf. The murkiness grabbed Jonah again and he wondered how he could comfortably conceal this latest secret from the monster of suspicion now prowling in the parlours of Western Shore.

But if he told, he'd have to admit to treasure hunting—wouldn't he? He stared back at the island. Did he imagine the waving branch or was that really Charlotte's flowing hair camouflaged in the lower branches of a birch tree?

A grinning Beaz tied his laces together and slung his shoes around his neck. "So, Mr. Steevens," he said. "Where's your car parked?"

For a split second, the teacher stopped rowing.

CHAPTER 13

SUNDAY CAME AND WENT, AND JONAH HAD stuffed his face at the church potluck. He even ate five of the Wharf Prophet's devilled eggs. It didn't help. He was stopped up like a tailpipe with a sock in it.

"Anything yet?" Beaz asked Monday afternoon.

"Stop asking," Jonah said. "Can't go under pressure."

And he couldn't. It was a family trait on his mother's side. Jonah wasn't sure how he knew this, he just did. To "go" in a timely fashion, he needed ideal conditions: no stress, home court advantage, etc.

"What are you going to do with it? Strain it through chicken wire?"

"That's not helping, Beaz." Jonah suspected he knew exactly why he was a bucket of nerves. To go *in* the toilet or *not* in the toilet—that was the question. He had an old washbasin shoved under his bed just in case, but it all seemed so…prehistoric, and *not* ideal.

"Let's go for a bike ride."

"Sure," Jonah said. "Not too far, though. Just in case."

They spun around the wharf, the schoolhouse parking lot, and in front of the general store.

"We should look for it."

"For what?" Jonah asked suspiciously. Beaz was sounding downright bonkers now. There's no way anyone would get to poke *anywhere* near that locket!

"Mr. Steevens' car."

"Oh." Envisioning the baby blue beast the last time he saw it, with Charlotte's hair waving in the wind, Jonah asked, "Why?"

Beaz shrugged. "Bored, I guess. Our boat's gone so we can't treasure hunt. But if we just sit around and do nothing, it's a waste." He laughed. "Get it, a *waste*? As in *waste product*."

"Funny."

"Come on! Crandall's Point Road isn't that far away on our bikes."

"You think that's where the car is?"

"Where else could it be?"

On Saturday, Mr. Steevens hadn't answered Beaz's question about his car. Instead, their teacher had clamped his lips together and resumed rowing twice as fast. He'd practically shoved the boys out of the boat and onto dry land, whipping back across the water like he was fleeing the scene of a crime.

"But we didn't see the car when we looked for it on Saturday," Jonah said.

Popping a wheelie on his bike, Beaz said, "Yeah, but we didn't look very long, remember? You only had one shoe."

"Of course I remember!" The walk back to Western Shore had added more blisters to Jonah's growing summer collection of minor injuries. Then he had had to explain his missing pants and shoe.

His story was that his clothing was carried off with the tide while he was swimming—all *sort of* true. After his mom growled at him to be more careful around the water and to take an adult with them next time, she loaded up his supper plate with a mountain of hodgepodge. Beaz was right; Jonah's mother took out all her frustrations in the kitchen.

Under the glare of the afternoon sun, they pedalled along the highway and veered left at Crandall's Point Road. Jonah's stomach gurgled and groaned as he struggled to keep up with Beaz.

"Look for tire tracks!" Beaz said.

Zipping up and down the road, they stopped anywhere it looked like the bushes had been recently disturbed. They found nothing.

Jonah's insides lurched like a tidal wave and he let one rip. "Gotta go," he said.

"Sure, let's head back," Beaz agreed. "First priority, get that locket back. Bet it's worth a bazillion dollars."

Jonah shook his head and jumped off his bike. "Not go home. Gotta go *now*! Here!" Darting into the woods, Jonah found a clump of trees to hide behind. "Stay away!" he yelled back. "I mean it!"

Standing up a few minutes later, Jonah caught a glimpse of shimmering blue through the spruce trees. "Beaz?" he called.

"I'm not anywhere near you!"

"Come here," Jonah said. "I'm done and I just found it."

Branches cracked as Beaz thrashed through the forest. "You've got the locket," he whooped.

Jonah frowned. Apparently Beaz wasn't as accurate as he used to be at reading his mind. "Mr. Steevens' car," he clarified. "Over there."

"What about the locket?" Beaz said, sniffing the air. "I know you went."

Heat scorched Jonah's face. "I checked. Don't ask. But the locket is still playing 'hide and go seek' in my gut."

"Gotcha," Beaz said. "So let's go look at the car, then."

They crept through the trees silently, as if sneaking up on a wild animal.

The car doors were locked. But there on the front seat was a lunch box—painted with pink and white daisies.

"It's Charlotte's."

Jonah agreed. He stumbled away from the car, searching for a place to sit. Charlotte's parents were worried enough about her running off with the teacher to involve the RCMP. Whatever was going on, her parents deserved to know how close by she really was, didn't they? It wasn't like Mr. Steevens and Charlotte had gotten married. Gulping, Jonah said, "We gotta tell someone."

"I know," Beaz said. "I think that's why I wanted to look for the car. We can tell the Mounties that we found it and let them figure out the rest."

"It's perfect!" Jonah said. "Then no one has to know about us going to the island."

"That's what I was thinking."

Crashing back through the trees, they jumped on their bikes.

"Wait!" Jonah yelled, jamming on his brakes.

Beaz skidded his back wheel. "What?" he shouted back.

"He might tell," Jonah said. Cold fingers of fear wrapped their way around his insides again. "If they find him, Mr. Steevens might tell the police that we were there."

"Oh," Beaz stammered. "Well...maybe...do you think Charlotte's all right, then?"

"Sure...it's not like she's his prisoner or anything. After all, I saw her choose to get in the car with him."

"Right."

"So we're back to saying nothing?" Jonah asked.

"Nothing. Sounds good to me." Gravel flew as Beaz whipped up Crandall's Point Road.

Jonah's stomach somersaulted like he'd spent two days and nights trapped on an out-of-control tilt-a-whirl at the Bill Lynch Show.

Stupid locket.

Stupid teacher.

Stupid everything.

Time for the unthinkable.

Prunes.

CHAPTER 14

BETTY SCHOFIELD NEVER LET ANYONE BUY ON store credit. It was rumoured that even the Pope, his eminent self, would have to pay cash at the general store. She ran a tab for one of her sons, though—pasted on the refrigerator door in her private kitchen.

Jonah had never been beyond the wainscotted walls of the store into the personal domain of Mrs. Schofield, but Ruth MacDonald had stopped in for tea at Betty's on Sunday afternoon—and now she was making the rounds, telling the whole neighbourhood about "the list."

"There's only one for Tom," Ruth cackled, when she stopped in to see Jonah's mom Tuesday morning.

Muriel Morgan tried to look busy, whipping up a batch of gingerbread. "I just have a few minutes today, Ruth. I have to take Jonah to the dentist in Chester."

"One stick of gum!" Ruth said. "And she writes it down! Where's the list for that lazy, no-good drifter other son of hers, Benny? Tom's the responsible one and he's got to pay her back for the pop she gives him once a week! And that's *after* he mows her lawn."

Jonah scraped the bowl and licked gingerbread batter off the spoon.

"Wasteful!" Ruth muttered, sounding just as stingy as Betty Schofield. "You left half the batter in there for that boy to slurp."

Jonah's mother sighed. "It's hardly half, Ruth. Jonah likes the batter; it's his favourite part. What difference does it make if he eats it raw or cooked?"

Suddenly, Ruth paid attention to Jonah. "Do you have a job this summer? It's not good for young men to be idle, you know, Muriel."

"I have chores," Jonah mumbled.

"How old are you?"

"Fourteen."

"And no job?" Ruth shook her head. "I know you only have the *one* child now, and Abraham makes a good living..." She stopped, her eyes darting around and blinking at the sparkling new kitchen appliances. Then her neck twisted to stare at the Royal Albert displayed in the china hutch.

Jonah saw her lips move as she counted the twelve place settings. The envy spreading over her countenance was as plain as the nose on her wrinkly face. Ruth MacDonald's daughters worked like slaves in the community. No job was too small and no nickel was refused. *She's not cheap like Betty Schofield,* he thought, *but she wants what everyone else has.*

She whipped her head back. "You have to give more thought to his character. After all, his brother…"

Jonah's mom slammed the metal pan onto the counter. "Air bubbles," she said with a tight smile on her face. "Jonah, go get washed up and changed."

His belly rumbled as he jumped into a freshly pressed pair of trousers. He'd eaten seven prunes the night before and gagged with every one. Just thinking about their sticky, slimy texture made him dry heave again now. They were a last resort, those prunes, but he wanted that locket out.

"Your father is working in his study, so he can watch the gingerbread," Jonah's mom said at his bedroom door a moment later. "I need to freshen up and then we can go."

Jonah's family had two vehicles and a television set. They were the only ones in Western Shore to have either of those luxuries. His dad often worked from home, but if he needed to visit a client then Jonah's mom still had the convenience of her own car to run errands.

"That woman!" Muriel Morgan exclaimed a few minutes later as they headed toward Chester. "The nerve of her telling me how to raise my child! There's not a darn thing wrong with your character."

The prunes slid around Jonah's intestines. He'd never spent so much time absorbed in the workings of his digestive system. "I think she's jealous of you."

His mom relaxed her grip on the steering wheel. "I never thought about that," she said. She reached out and patted him on the arm. "Maybe you're right. And wise, too. I'm proud of you."

Guilt swirled in his stomach, playing tag with the prunes and locket. What would his mother say if she knew where he'd been? Knew what he knew? "Thanks," he said.

"Let's stop for an ice cream."

"What about the dentist? Won't I be late?"

"We're early," his mom admitted sheepishly. "Just an hour, or so. In my defence, I couldn't stand to have Ruth in my kitchen a minute longer. Besides, I didn't exactly say what time we had to be there…"

Jonah smiled. Maybe his mom would understand his dilemma after all. "Double scoop of butterscotch swirl, please."

"Manners and everything. Did I raise my boy right, or what?"

The best place to get ice cream in Chester was at the gas station. Jonah remembered that just as his mother pulled into the parking lot.

Marshall gave them a curt nod from beside the gas pump.

"Strange boy," Jonah's mom whispered. "Nice one minute, a holy terror the next."

Jonah appreciated how his mom always spoke her mind and didn't talk down to him. Before Caleb had been born, she had been the teacher at Western Shore's one-room schoolhouse—even Ruth MacDonald never had a bad thing to report about Muriel Morgan's teaching days. She'd been a community favourite who "retired" when she became a mom.

"I taught Marshall's brother, Deacon, you know. The whole family seems...intense."

"Marshall's a bit of a bully if you get on his wrong side."

His mom raised her eyebrows. "He hasn't been picking on you, has he?"

"Nope. I stay on his right side."

"Good."

"Did you know Marshall and Caleb were friends?" Jonah held his breath. He didn't often mention his brother's name.

She sucked in air like she'd been punched. "No. Not really...maybe...let's get our ice cream, okay?"

Jonah ordered his double scoop and his mom ordered a single scoop of strawberry. They ate at a picnic table under a shady maple.

"You owe me for that ice cream. Ten cents," his mom said a few minutes later, opening her handbag and taking out a pen and notebook. "I'm starting a list, for your character."

They both burst out laughing and Marshall stared at them, scowling.

Jonah glanced away and dug into the second scoop of his double-decker cone. The frozen sugary butterscotch melted on his tongue. "I'm getting full," he said as his stomach gave another tidal-wavish lurch. "I need the bathroom. Number two."

Jumping up, he darted into the gas station. "The key," he panted. "Hurry."

The clerk handed over the key chained to a block of wood. "Stupid kids. Don't make a mess in there," he growled.

Jonah ran outside and jogged to the back of the station. Hopping from foot to foot, he jiggled the key in the lock. "Come on, open!"

He raced inside and slammed the door. Not the toilet, he thought, looking around the cramped, smelly cubicle. He spied a dirt-splattered mop bucket.

A few minutes later, he pulled up his drawers and stared at the mushy mound in the bucket. Things were a little runny thanks to all those prunes. With relief he saw a shiny speck of gold—no treasure hunting required.

The locket.

But he still had to fish it out somehow.

He propped the bathroom door open with his foot. "Where's a stick when you need it?"

A few feet away lay the perfect one! He reached for it and his foot slipped. "No!" he shouted as the door slammed before he could grab onto the handle.

"Dang," he whispered, pacing back and forth. "Dang. Dang. Dang!" It was like he'd invented a new song—the "Triple Dang, I'm in a Load of Trouble" hoedown.

"Ready?" his mom said, peeking her head around the corner. "I was about to send a search party."

Jonah gulped. "Not yet. I locked the key inside."

"I'm sure they have another one. I'll tell the clerk when I get a fill up."

"No!" Jonah shouted. His face flamed. "I...forgot to... flush."

"Oh for heaven's sake. I'll see if there's another key."

A moment later she returned. "The clerk wasn't too pleased."

"Great." Jonah grabbed the key in one hand and a stick in the other. He wondered how pleased the clerk would have been to discover the mop bucket.

Marshall Delray would have blabbed the news all the way to Bridgewater and back...or at least left a note...

Back inside the foul-smelling bathroom, Jonah knew he'd never tell another living soul about this moment— not even Beaz. When he was done lathering soap on the locket, he dried it off on a grimy towel hanging by the sink. "It's so shiny now," he whispered, looking at his distorted reflection in the gold.

Who knew? The treasure had taken a three-day joyride through his stomach and intestines and came out the other end polished like it had been buffed at the jewellers.

Now, where to put it until he could show it to Beaz?

Thankfully, his trousers had deep pockets.

Then he cleaned out the bucket and washed his hands—soaping them up *three* times before he sniffed and decided the odour was gone.

When he came back outside, his mom had the car pulled up to the pump and Marshall was filling the tank. "Looks like rain," Marshall said, staring at the dark clouds drifting in from the west.

Jonah stared. In a matter of moments, the air had transformed into a heavy dampness that hung like an invisible curtain.

"Thunder and lightning," his mom said, sighing as she paid for the gas. "Darn! My geraniums are in for a beating. I hope Dad thinks to bring the pots in off the veranda."

Jonah shrugged. His mother was a whiz in the kitchen, but her thumb was permanently black. More than likely, those geraniums were already dead.

CHAPTER 15

Victoria Hails' screams could be heard up and down the highway from the general store all the way to Gold River. During every thunder and lightning storm, she'd stand on her porch and cry out into the rain.

"Mrs. Hails really wails," Beaz said.

"Ha, ha," Jonah laughed artificially. The joke was an old one and *not* a Beaz original.

The middle-aged Mrs. Hails had been noticeably terrified of thunder and lightning ever since her third husband went out in a storm and never came back. She wore her cascading grey-streaked hair down to her waist and dressed in widow's black, but all of the community knew there had been no body.

"I think Mr. Hails ran away," Beaz said.

"You and the rest of the South Shore," Jonah said. He rolled the dice and scooted the metal boot around the game board. "I passed 'Go.' That'll be two hundred bucks, please."

Banker Beaz doled out the dough. "I'm gonna be bankrupt again in a minute."

The power had gone out not long after the storm started. Jonah's mom had stopped to pick Beaz up for a sleepover on the way back from Chester and they'd been stuck in the candlelit kitchen with Jonah's parents, playing board games. Jonah thought he'd burst waiting to tell Beaz the news.

"Time for bed soon," Jonah's dad said.

"Can we have a candle?" asked Jonah.

"Take this," his mom said, reaching for the hurricane lamp on the windowsill. "But be careful with it."

Up in Jonah's room, Beaz unfolded the extra quilts to make up a bed on the floor. "Bet Mr. Steevens is taking a pounding over on the island."

"Shh," Jonah whispered. "I have it." He took out the locket from his pocket and held it up to the flickering glow of the lamp.

"Holy hillbilly," Beaz whispered back. "What did you do to it, shine it up with lemon oil?"

"Nope." Jonah grinned. "Came out that way."

"You're kidding. All by itself!"

"Of course not! I had to wash it off first."

Beaz wrinkled his nose and sniffed. "You washed it good, right?"

"Just get it over with," Jonah said. "Do a poop joke so it's out of your system."

"Hey, that's a good one, 'out of your system.'"

"Funny," Jonah said wryly. He ran his finger over the side of the locket. Now that it was polished up, even in the dim light he could see the tiny latch mechanism. "I think it opens here."

It took a moment, but finally the pirate's treasure cracked open to reveal its ancient secret. "A photo," Jonah said through clamped lips. He secretly feared the locket might spontaneously take flight and fling itself back down his digestive tract.

"Let me see," Beaz said. He held it up to the lamp. "There's a woman on one side and a man on the other."

Jonah squinted at the picture and felt his heart hammer in tune with the pelting rain against the window. "That's no woman, Beaz. That's Charlotte Barkhouse!"

"Who's the man? Mr. Steevens?"

Pulling the locket closer, Jonah stared at the photo. "It's blurry," he said. "Water must have seeped in when I washed it. I guess it could be him."

"You know what that means?" Beaz sighed.

"Yup. This ain't no pirate's treasure."

"Not a chance," Beaz mumbled. "Our boat sank and now we've found something as worthless as fool's gold. We must be cursed."

The storm raged its wildest at high tide near midnight. Jonah woke through the night as the window panes rattled. The wind howled until dawn broke. Or maybe it was more wailing from Mrs. Hails. Either way, Jonah watched the blaze of sunrise with sleep in his eyes. His body felt like dead weight.

Random parts of the highway hugging the shoreline were littered with seaweed and rotting fish. The angry waves had even scattered debris from the ocean into the ditch on the opposite side of the road. Jonah sunk his chin into his hands and stared out his bedroom window.

Yesterday, his father had rescued the geraniums from the rain, but now he wondered who would rescue the flowers from his mother's deadly care after she placed them back out in today's sunlight.

"Need your help, boys," Abraham Morgan said an hour later over breakfast. "Quite a few branches down in our yard."

"Beaz has to check the coop first," Jonah said. "And I promised to help."

"Fine. Just get at it soon. Rake up the leaves, too, please."

The hens screeched almost as loud as Mrs. Hails had the night before.

"They sure are worked up," Beaz said. He fastened the latch on a shutter that had broken loose in the wind. "Only two eggs this morning and both of them smashed to smithereens." He tidied up the straw and put out more food and water.

They walked back to Jonah's and started gathering the branches strewn across the lawn. "I can't believe we didn't find pirate gold," Jonah grumbled. "How did Charlotte's stupid locket end up in the Money Pit?"

"Maybe that's why they're hiding out over there. Hunting for Captain Kidd's treasure," Beaz said. "Mr. Steevens did spend an awful lot of time talking about pirates."

"What about Charlotte?" Jonah said, his eyebrows raised. "Do you think she shimmied down in that shaft with her perfect stockings and high heels?" Even as he said it, he cringed. He was reminded of how mussed her clothing had looked when she'd climbed into Mr. Steevens' car.

"Good point. Maybe it fell in by accident, then."

"I guess," Jonah said. "The chain must have broken."

"Did you see a chain anywhere?"

"Nothing," Jonah answered. "Probably at the bottom with the worms." He took two rakes from the shed and they brushed away the twigs and leaves. "Do you even remember Charlotte wearing a gold locket?"

"I don't know."

Thinking about her that last day in school, Jonah pictured her trotting to the front of the class and reciting her poem. "She tugged at something around her neck when she read that weird death poem."

"Yeah," Beaz exclaimed. "I bet this was it!" His face turned pale. "You don't think she fell down there, do you? Dead?"

Remembering the light glinting off Charlotte's blond hair on the island, Jonah said, "Not a chance. I saw her when we were rowing back. She was standing in the trees. Watching us."

"Mystery solved, then," Beaz said, still looking unusually whitish-green as he added, "Mom is coming home a week early. This Saturday. I didn't want to tell you last night and ruin your shiny-clean-locket news."

Slumping over the handle of the rake, Jonah stared across the road at the schoolhouse. Seagulls swarmed above the building, alternating nosedives into the rosebushes behind it.

The summer had ended before it even started. The *Gingerale* was gone. The Money Pit was an empty tomb of dirt, worms, and wood. And, the final nail in the treasure-hunting coffin—Mrs. Hodder was coming home early.

"Let's go down Vaughn Road," Jonah suggested. He was sick of his gloomy thoughts. "Maybe the storm washed up something good."

Beaz's eyes widened. "Like the *Gingerale*?"

"Maybe." Jonah shrugged.

This time Jonah knew for sure that the eyes of Western Shore were watching. After a storm, neighbours gathered outside comparing stories of damage and power outages while sharing mugs of tea brewed over their wood stoves.

"A teddy bear," Beaz shouted a few minutes later, lifting

a lump of soggy black and white fur off the rocks at the beach. "A panda."

Combing the shoreline, Jonah felt restless. A week into summer and the disappointment weighted him. He sat down on a flat boulder and kicked the rocks. The water lapped a few feet away and a piece of floating driftwood caught his eye. "Beaz," he said. "Come here!"

The heaviness sunk to the depths of his stomach. "Look," he said, pointing to the curved wood clanking against the rocks.

"Oh," Beaz said, looking as if he might cry.

The green paint on the wood was faded, but the crude black letters stood out boldly in the sun: *Gingerale.*

"She's not even in one piece anymore." Jonah pulled the lonely remnant of their craft out of the water and stared across the bay at Oak Island. There was no smoke this morning—no signs of life.

"Let's go fishing," Beaz said.

Jonah fastened the remainder of their watercraft to his handlebars with a piece of rope he found nearby. The *Gingerale*'s final resting place would be his old fort, back behind the apple tree. "Ready," he said.

His front wheel wobbled under the weight of the wood as he peddled home. They nailed the plank over the doorway of the fort and gathered up their fishing gear.

From the wharf, Jonah could see human scavengers

strolling the shore, searching for treasures coughed up by the sea. The noon sun beat down and Jonah smelled the rotting fish. "Funny," he said. "There must be something big behind the schoolhouse. A tuna or a whale maybe? Whatever it is, it must be huge. The gulls have been circling over there all morning."

The Wharf Prophet strolled by and Jonah studied the old fisherman's face. It seemed that Sam Cooke also had his eyes on the gulls.

"I think the fish are just as mixed up as Mom's hens," Beaz said. "Nothing's biting."

"I wonder what's going on over there." Jonah pointed to the gathering crowd in the schoolhouse parking lot. He heard shouts and saw Ruth MacDonald run across the road in her slippers.

Beaz shrugged. "You're right. Something big must've washed up. Let's go see!"

They rounded the schoolhouse and Jonah saw the Wharf Prophet's hands held up. "Everybody back," he yelled. "Keep clear until the constable gets here."

Jonah pushed to the front of the spectators and stared at the ground beneath the rosebushes.

The sweater.

The skirt.

The hair.

The sea had coughed up Charlotte Barkhouse.

CHAPTER 16

IT WAS WRONG TO STARE AT HER FEET. EVEN though Jonah knew it, he couldn't stop. The second toe on her right foot sprouted freakishly long like a jointed string bean and rested on top of the crooked big toe.

"It's like *Invasion of the Body Snatchers*," Jonah whispered.

Beaz raised his eyebrows. "Huh?"

Jonah stared back at the toes. "Alien feet," he whispered.

Beaz snorted.

A chorus of "shh" amongst disapproving frowns forced Jonah to suck in the sides of his cheeks and bite down hard. *Don't laugh*, he told himself with his cheeks pulled in. *And don't think about how you now have fish lips.*

Once again, Betty Schofield stood before the community on tiptoe in high heels. But this time they ·were open-toed sandals fresh from the summer Simpsons-Sears catalogue. And because Jonah and Beaz had somehow managed to be shoved to the front of the mob when they all poured into the schoolhouse for another hastily called meeting, the two boys were sitting cross-legged on the floor, "nose to toes" with Betty's feet.

"It must be from wearing all those pointy-toed stilts," Beaz whispered.

Bite. Bite. Bite.

For a second, Jonah thought he tasted blood, he was chomping on his cheeks so hard.

"The constable will talk to us as soon as Char...," Betty paused. "The body is taken away."

Not even the bees buzzed now. The hushed schoolhouse was paying its due to the loss of one of its own.

Charlotte's friend Jenny broke the silence with a groaning sob.

"We don't need Deacon Delray to tell us what we already know," Ruth MacDonald snarled. "That teacher did this."

Threats of revenge mixed with the rising tide of tears.

Abraham Morgan stood and cleared his throat. "The man's innocent until we can prove him otherwise."

Jonah squirmed. He could feel the crowd shift a portion of their anger toward the one who dared to contradict them. And for the first time in his life, Jonah knew that he, too, sided against the words spoken by his father.

Because Mr. Steevens *was* guilty.

"The man's a maniac," Ruth said. "And he's on the loose."

The constable's boots pounded up the wooden steps. "I'll take it from here, Betty," he said as he strode to the front of the schoolroom.

Staring up from the floor, Jonah noticed for the first time how much Deacon and Marshall resembled one another. Something about the way their chins dominated their faces...or maybe it was just Jonah's current point of view, looking up like a bug from the floor.

"As many of you may have already guessed, Charlotte is no longer missing."

Jenny cried out again and then stumbled over the tangled legs in the crowded room to run outside.

"She was...a beautiful girl...and will be...missed." The constable cleared his throat. "We will try to determine the approximate time of death as soon as possible."

Jonah wondered if he had really seen Charlotte's hair fluttering in the trees on Oak Island or if it had been an illusion. Was he the last person other than Mr. Steevens to see her alive?

The schoolhouse door creaked open again and Jonah peered down the aisle—Deacon's mirror image, Marshall, stood with his hands in his pockets. The news of Charlotte must have already travelled to the Chester gas station and beyond. It was the second time he had shown up tardy to a town meeting.

Constable Delray cleared his throat. "According to her

parents, Charlotte has on the same clothing she wore the day she disappeared. If anyone saw anything that day or later, come forward now. Even the smallest bit of a clue could help in the investigation."

"I saw something," Marshall said, his lips in a thin red line.

"Marshall?" The constable's neck stained with a scarlet flush. "What haven't you told me?"

"He knows too," Marshall said, nodding to the front of the room.

Jonah wished he were a tiny crumb on the floor that could be carried off by an ant or a mouse. He wasn't. Instead he was a fourteen-year-old boy seated at the feet of a towering, steel-toed-boot-wearing Mountie.

"This kid?" Constable Delray said, the flush fading to a pale pink. He seemed relieved to have the attention pulled away from Marshall.

Now Jonah felt and *saw* everyone's eyes on him. His father's, his mother's, and Beaz...Beaz looked like he was about to barf.

What did Marshall want him to say?

"Yeah, um, like I said, I saw them together...in the car."

"What about before that?" Marshall sneered. "At the school?"

Traitor, Jonah thought.

"Oh yeah…they came out of the school together." Jonah's voice squeaked.

"They were in there alone?" the constable snapped. "If both of you knew, why didn't you mention it before?"

Because I would have died of embarrassment?

Marshall shrugged. "Didn't seem important. You already knew Charlotte had run off with him."

"Anything else?" The scarlet stripe was back across the constable's neck.

Jonah knew Marshall was staring at him—waiting. He wished he could rat out the big dumbbell, just for revenge. "No."

Would Marshall back him up or would he mention the note?

For the first time Marshall lost some of his swagger. "Nothing."

What would the crowd be thinking now if they knew about the note? Something like, *It's no big deal, poor kid, threatened by a bully to drop off a harmless note. No wonder he didn't say any more about it. The big oaf told the kid not to read it. The kid didn't even tell his best friend about it.*

But Jonah had read it and he had seen Mr. Steevens and Charlotte tear out of the parking lot. It was time for Jonah to face the truth. This might have been the moment he crossed over an invisible line—the one marked "lie."

And what about the island? What about knowing where a murderer was hiding?

Constable Delray cleared his throat. It was obvious he was embarrassed to be interrogating his own flesh and blood in front of the whole community. "You knew more about this relationship and didn't tell me?"

Marshall shrugged. "Sure. Anyone with eyeballs could see him mooning over her at school."

"What about you, Jonah? Did you see anything inappropriate during the school hours?"

"Not really, sir. Like Beaz said to you the other day, he called her 'dear' once." *Twice.*

Jonah wondered if everyone did this, listened to the words of a question and only answered what was asked.

The school hours had ended when the bell rang last Thursday afternoon—everything else Jonah knew had happened *after* that. Only Beaz knew that he'd been *in* the school. Only Beaz knew what he'd seen...or *thought* he saw. Only Beaz knew about Jonah swallowing the locket.

Hairs prickled on his arms. Only *Marshall* knew about giving Jonah the note. Was he hiding more stuff too?

"Mr. Marcus Steevens is our prime suspect," Deacon Delray said, clenching his teeth until his jaw muscles bulged. "I want to be the first to hear any information you might have, is that clear?"

As clear as Oak Island dirt, Jonah thought, folding and unfolding his hands. There was one more thing only he and Beaz knew—they had been rescued from Oak Island by Deacon Delray's prime suspect.

Mumbling a quick goodnight to Beaz, Jonah ran home. He stared at the *Gingerale*'s name nailed above the doorway to his fort. He'd inherited the half-shack, half-shed after Caleb's death.

"You wouldn't keep a secret like this, would you?" he whispered to his phantom brother. He expected no answer other than the one he could dream up for himself—Caleb did no wrong.

Jumping on his bike, he pedalled by the light of the moon. His mother would be furious to know he was riding after dark. He ended up in a clump of trees near the Dine and Dance—another infraction if his mother got wind of it. Not that he'd go inside. He simply liked listening to the music that drifted out through the screened windows in summer. Besides, it was only a little after 9:00 p.m. and the sun had just set. The real trouble didn't start until well after midnight.

After listening to a couple of songs, he sped home, knowing his mother would be looking for him. Rounding the last corner, he jammed on his brakes.

Deacon Delray's car was in the driveway.

Jonah careened up the neighbour's driveway and

crept around to the back of his own yard. What was the constable doing here again?

He stashed his bike behind the fort and held his breath.

They were talking, his dad and the constable.

"I need your help," the constable said. "You still owe me."

"I know," Abraham Morgan said.

For the first time ever, Jonah heard shame in his father's voice.

CHAPTER 17

BEAZ'S MOTHER DIDN'T COME HOME AS PLANNED on Saturday. His grandmother took a turn for the worse and Mrs. Hodder insisted that Beaz join her in Halifax for a few days. Apparently the big city streets were far more civilized; dead bodies weren't currently being washed up in Halifax Harbour.

"You should bury the locket," Beaz said. It was early Sunday morning and he'd met Jonah in the old fort to say goodbye before driving to the city.

The sun had faithfully appeared every day after Charlotte's body had surfaced on Tuesday, but an ominous cloud of dread had sat on Jonah's shoulders since seeing her lifeless body in the rosebushes and the constable's car repeatedly in his driveway. "They're looking for Mr. Steevens and we know where he is," Jonah said. "Constable Delray's been here three times to get Dad's advice. And I don't know what's wrong with my dad…he barely eats…"

"They'll find the car. We did."

They'd had this conversation at least a dozen times a day, *every* day, since Charlotte had washed ashore.

"They think he's in Ontario, Beaz. They're not even really looking for him here."

"Why not?" Beaz said. "She died during the storm. How fast could he get away?"

Jonah shook his head. "She didn't. Last night I overheard the constable tell Dad she'd been dead for days. Probably since the last day of school."

"Holy hillbilly!" Beaz wrung his hands. "We took a boat ride with a murderer!"

"I know."

"But you said you saw her on Saturday. In the trees!"

"I saw...someone."

Beaz lowered his head. "We gotta say something, don't we."

It wasn't a question. Beaz just stated it, plain and simple, and Jonah knew that his best friend spoke the truth. They were in over their heads in a truckload of trouble. At first everyone thought Charlotte had just run off—it wasn't like anyone was even calling it a kidnapping. But now...

"What about an anonymous note about the car?" Jonah whispered, realizing he couldn't even take credit for his idea. He'd stolen it from the lame brain Marshall Delray. "I could mail it to the RCMP."

"Postmarked the general store?" Beaz sounded dubious. "What if someone sees you?"

"Western Shore is spilling over with people," Jonah said. "No one will see me. Betty Schofield is selling ice cream sundaes and everything. She's telling everyone plain vanilla was Charlotte's favourite. That way she can charge the same but skimp on toppings."

Since Tuesday, Western Shore had become a popular tourist attraction. Folks came from as far away as Yarmouth to view the lonely deathbed of Charlotte Barkhouse. A smiling photo of her had been plastered on the front page of daily newspapers all across Nova Scotia. Beside Charlotte's dazzling image was a bug-eyed photo of Marcus Steevens with the caption: "Have You Seen this Man?"

Betty Schofield was cashing in.

"But Charlotte never ate ice cream there. No one did before Tuesday."

"It's called bending the truth, Beaz. I'm starting to think everyone does it a little."

"But some things snap if they're bent too far," Beaz said. He twisted his ball cap in his hands. "Do they know how Charlotte died? Did she drown?" He sounded hopeful, like maybe it was all just one big unfortunate accident.

"The Mounties aren't telling the papers yet," Jonah said slowly. He remembered what he'd heard last night when the constable had sworn his father to secrecy about the details of the case.

"You know, don't you?" Beaz said. "Spill it. Who else am I going to tell?"

"They think she was strangled with something thin and metal."

"Oh…ohh," Beaz whimpered. "Don't tell me."

"They're not sure," Jonah said. "But Charlotte's parents said she had a chain with a locket on it and now it's missing. The police are keeping that quiet." Even as he said it, the full impact of the revelation hit Jonah harder than an atom bomb.

"Ohh…" Beaz slid into a heap on the dusty floor.

It welled up in Jonah, the dark secret they were keeping. "I swallowed half of the murder weapon," he said. "And now it's stuffed away in my underwear drawer."

"We're going straight to hell," Beaz said, rocking back and forth. "And I don't even know much about hell but I've got a feeling it's for kids like us."

Jonah shuddered. He'd been so careful not to tell a lie. They'd wrangled their way out of confessing about sailing to Oak Island, nearly drowning in the bay, and losing their clothing. Even Beaz had managed to explain his missing pants to his dad.

But withholding evidence in a murder investigation? If lying sent you to hell and stealing landed you in the extra-crispy section, what did being an accomplice to murder do?

"I'm thirsty," Jonah said, licking his parched lips. "Really thirsty."

"Beaz!" Mr. Hodder shouted from the Morgans' driveway. "Let's get going."

"Sure, Dad," Beaz croaked, hauling himself off of the floor.

"Thanks for looking after the hens for a few days," Mr. Hodder called out to Jonah. "We'll be back on Wednesday night."

"Yup," Jonah said reluctantly. It was a part of his self-imposed penance, tending to Beaz's chicken coop. He'd rather wash floors for a nickel than muck around in that stuffy, stinky shed.

"The Captain wants a dozen delivered," Beaz reminded him. "And that's besides the other three deliveries."

Perfect, Jonah thought. Now he had to deliver the Wharf Prophet's eggs all by himself. He closed his eyes, trying to drive away the image of Sam Cooke waving the crowd away from the rosebushes while Charlotte's twisted body lay at his feet. What did the Wharf Prophet know about Charlotte's death?

He was about to drive his bike to Beaz's when he ran back up to his room. The locket was still stuffed in the back of his top drawer, balled up in a rumpled handkerchief.

"You're coming with me," he whispered, sticking it in his pants pocket.

All the way to the chicken coop, Jonah's thigh felt like it was burning. Maybe the locket was giving off its own hellfire and brimstone.

Quickly he gathered the eggs and watered and fed the hens. One of the birds pecked at his toe. "Shove off," he said, moving the hen away with a gentle kick. The sudden movement loosened the handkerchief from his pocket and the locket thudded to the floor.

Jonah stared. It was as if the locket was daring him to deny its existence. Picking it up, he wrapped the handkerchief around it once again. He needed time to think about what to do. Maybe he could drop it in the rosebushes behind the schoolhouse and the police would find it? Or maybe it could mysteriously appear one night after another rainstorm?

He knew it wasn't safe anymore in his underwear drawer. He thought about the days it had travelled through his midsection—really that locket wasn't safe anywhere near him, the ill-fated Jonah Morgan.

A board squeaked under his shoe and Jonah bent down to see if he could pry it up. With a quick tug, it sprung free. "Just for a day or two," he whispered, pressing the handkerchief into the damp soil underneath. "Until I have a chance to figure out what to do with you."

With the eggs balanced in the wire basket, he headed toward Sam Cooke's lopsided shanty. How could one solitary man need so many eggs?

The door opened before Jonah had even had a chance to knock. "Come in," the gruff Wharf Prophet said. Today his hair was tamed and his eyes were clear.

Jonah glanced at the old fisherman's hands—leathered but not smeared in blood.

"Sit down." Sam Cooke pointed to a well-worn rocker beside the kitchen woodstove.

The room had a kept feeling, as if everything was placed just so. But faded: the hooked rug in front of the sink had lost its crisp pattern and the china precisely displayed on the shelf showed signs of cracks and wear.

The Wharf Prophet pulled a chair up to the kitchen table and rested his elbows while folding his hands in front of him. "Now Jonah," he said. "Tell me what you know about this here murder."

His breath smelled like pickled herring.

Jonah hated pickled herring.

And now he hated eggs, too. If it wasn't for Beaz's mother's stupid chicken coop and the Wharf Prophet's mammoth consumption of eggs, Jonah wouldn't be sliding down the slippery slope of telling the biggest whopper he'd ever told. "I don't...I don't know what you mean."

Sam Cooke combed at the whiskers in his beard with calloused fingers. "I saw the look on your face, boy."

"Water, please," Jonah croaked, afraid he might choke on his own saliva.

The old fisherman peered at Jonah for a moment before shuffling over to the sink. He ran the tap, swirling the water around inside the glass. "Well's deep here. Artesian. Most folks don't like to run their water in summer. Afraid their well will go dry. Not me."

"Thanks." Jonah gulped the water and an air bubble slid down his esophagus. He banged on his chest. "Good... cold."

"Now, let's get down to business. Everyone else stared at Charlotte's body in shock, like they didn't understand who or what it was. You knew. How?"

Jonah didn't know where to look. If Sam Cooke could predict the future, he was sure to spot a lie. "I recognized her clothes."

"Hmm...maybe." The old fisherman leaned back in his chair. "But you didn't seem surprised to see her. Everyone else thought that girl was a thousand miles away."

Shrugging, Jonah picked at an imaginary spot on the table. It wasn't like the Wharf Prophet could really read his mind.

Could he?

"I don't pay much attention to gossip," Jonah said.

"Me and Beaz have been doing a lot of fishing…and beachcombing."

"And maybe some sailing?"

A river of ice water gushed through Jonah's veins. Had Sam Cooke seen them out on the bay? "Huh?"

"Nothing," he said, standing up. "Thanks for the eggs."

"Sure."

"I'll take another dozen tomorrow."

Jonah gulped. "Great." He sprinted down the driveway with the eggs for other deliveries jostling in the basket. Maybe it wasn't safe to come here anymore, doling out eggs to the Wharf Prophet—that kooky old man was off his rocker.

And sliding very close to the truth.

CHAPTER 18

MORE THAN A HUNDRED YEARS AGO, EDGAR Allan Poe had penned "The Tell-Tale Heart." As Jonah stepped over the floorboard in the chicken coop, he recalled the story. There wasn't a *tick, tick* coming from the locket, but he could feel its condemning presence while he fed and watered the hens.

Did Deacon Delray have the note yet?

Today was Tuesday, Charlotte's funeral. A week after her death, the police had finished with her body. They only released the vague detail that foul play was suspected.

The whole community would go to the event—it was a given. Owl-like eyes would scan the crowd, taking a visual attendance and report on who wore what, who sat with whom, and why on earth wasn't so-and-so there…

Jonah went.

It was his second funeral.

But it was his first time in the Anglican Church. Caleb's funeral had been at Bethel Mission in Martin's Point.

Jonah scratched at his neck under the stiffly pressed collar. July was too hot for suits and ties.

The casket was closed. He'd been afraid to see her again but soon overheard that there had been no "viewing" on account of the "decomposition."

Tick...

He swung his head to the back of the church where the grandfather clock kept a steady beat. Flies buzzed and landed on heads, on flowers, on the coffin.

The service was short.

The grandfather clock chimed eleven times as six solemn pallbearers shuffled down the aisle.

Still, Jonah felt sure he could hear the tick.

Marshall Delray walked in time with the other five— red-faced as he carried her, with sweat dripping near his ear. And also near his nose.

Or was that a tear?

Somehow in the procession to the graveside Jonah ended up beside Jenny.

"She was my best friend," Jenny whispered.

Being a year older than Jonah, Jenny usually never gave him the time of day. But here they were, both *best friendless*. His was in Halifax and hers was in…disposed.

"I'm sorry," Jonah said. He told himself that he wasn't responsible. He told himself that he couldn't have known what Mr. Steevens was capable of. He told himself…

Tick...

This time it wasn't really a *tick*, but a peck, a single peck before the knocking began in earnest...a woodpecker desecrating the morning.

"I don't understand why she left with him," Jenny said, wringing her hands.

She'd stopped and Jonah had stopped with her. The others pushed past like a surging tide. Jonah wanted to lift his feet and flow with them, away from Jenny. Away from her pain.

Tick...

Jonah fumbled for words. "Did you know...about them?"

Her mouth opened then closed. She shrugged, saying, "Charlotte sparkled. She was the closest thing to a star Western Shore is ever going to see. She had big dreams."

Wading through her reply, Jonah said, "You mean she wanted to leave here?"

"I don't know."

Jonah sighed. If Charlotte's best friend didn't know the truth...

He cringed, remembering he'd kept news of Marshall's note from Beaz and he suspected Beaz kept the severity of Mrs. Hodder's wrath hidden from him. So even best friends kept secrets.

"For a while she liked Marshall."

It explained things. Marshall's whistle when Charlotte strutted to the front of the classroom on that last day of school.

The note for the teacher.

The tear now.

"I saw them together, Mr. Steevens and her," Jonah said. "At the schoolhouse. I think they were kissing and maybe...I don't know...more?" He stopped. Why was he spilling his guts to her?

Her eyes bored into him. "Did you tell anyone that?"

"Just Beaz."

"Good. Keep it that way." She bit her lip. "Sometimes people...older boys...said things about Charlotte. Things that *weren't* true."

The funeral procession was far off now and the casket rested on the dirt mound beside the grave. Charlotte lay well beyond any further danger of physical harm but Jenny was still protecting—like best friends do.

"You don't think it matters?" Jonah said it with hope. Someone was giving him permission to keep quiet—secrecy was in Charlotte's best interest. He felt his stomach muscles relax.

Her shoulders slumped. "Not now. Nothing matters."

Tick, tick...

It was louder, more urgent. The woodpecker prompted what he already knew he needed to ask. "Who gave her the locket she had on that last day? Mr. Steevens?" He tried to act casual. She wouldn't know what he knew—the police suspected that that piece of jewellery was the murder weapon.

"I don't know," Jenny said. "Funny you happened to notice it too. I saw it on her chain for the very first time that day. She said she'd tell me all about it after school. But she never had a chance…" She swayed and her knees folded.

Jonah linked his arm through hers and pulled her along. The mourners were encircled around the graveside and the minister was speaking in a monotone drone. The two of them hung back, on the outskirts of the crowd, their arms still entwined. Jenny was fifteen and he was fourteen but age didn't seem to matter in the cemetery. Not today.

Today, two lonely souls had shared a secret.

CHAPTER 19

THE LADIES' AUXILIARY AT THE CHURCH SERVED crumb cakes, sandwiches, and tea. All the while, the sun beat down, turning the church hall into a sweltering oven. Not even a drop of lemonade. Who forgets lemonade at a church social?

Funeral, he corrected himself.

He raced home and tore off his suit and scratched at the hives on his arms and legs.

Torture.

The whole thing was torture.

Picking the suit back up, he smoothed it out and read the label—wool. His parents usually bought two new suits every year at Christmas for the school concert. He and Caleb would be dressed like matching singers in a quartet. The first Christmas after Caleb's death, Jonah had held his breath for a moment, wondering if instead of buying a new one, his parents would give him an old suit of Caleb's. They didn't. Caleb's suits had been whisked away somewhere mysterious—likely the missionary box.

Jonah shuddered in sympathy at the less fortunate folks in a painfully hot country being stuffed into wool suits. Two summers ago, and now again this summer, he'd worn his Christmas suits to funerals.

"Let me air that out," his mom said, appearing in the doorway.

He ducked behind his door. "Mom! I'm not dressed!"

"Oh for goodness' sake, I gave birth to you! Hand it over. I don't have all day."

Throwing the suit into the hallway, he slammed the door. What was he going to do for the rest of the day? Beaz really needed to get back home or the summer was going to be washed up.

Charlotte...

He pedalled toward Martin's Point and at the last second, with his heart hammering in his chest, he careened left and sped down Crandall's Point Road. Without meaning to, he ended up right where Mr. Steevens had parked his car. What if the Mounties had the note already?

It was gone!

Four sinkholes where the tires had recently wallowed in the mud were still visible—he had the right spot, but there was no car.

Now what? The police were about to receive a worthless clue.

It chewed at him again, the secrets he was keeping. Maybe it was time to tell someone…his father?

"What are *you* doing here?"

"I…I," Jonah stammered. Once more, he stared up into the square jaw of Deacon Delray. "I'm…nothing."

"Scram! Don't disturb the scene."

"Scene?" Jonah asked. He knew he should scram while the going was good, but he stood frozen like a statue.

Constable Delray frowned. "You're always turning up, aren't you? Abraham Morgan needs to keep better tabs on his kids…" his voice trailed off.

Kids? There was only one kid now…

Pink and white daisies winked from the bushes. "Oh," Jonah said, staring. Even with Deacon Delray watching, Jonah couldn't help it—bits of Charlotte were following him around and crying out to be noticed. "I think that's her lunch box," he mumbled.

"Da…dang," the constable said. "We got a tip this morning about a blue car here and we're too late. The rotter's gone!"

"A tip?" Jonah thought once again about the note he'd snuck into the mailbox outside the general store. He'd sandwiched it in between two letters his father was mailing to clients. That would have been his excuse if anyone had noticed him there.

The constable stared at Jonah. "Why are you here?" His eyes stayed focused. Unmoving.

Jonah remembered reading about snakes and how they were different than legless lizards—snakes didn't blink. He tried to keep his own eyes open and they burned, watering with tears. "I'm bored. Beaz is away."

"Stay out of my way! Your father acts like his kids are some sort of royalty—untouchable. But I've got proof…"

Jonah blinked. Hard. What did Deacon Delray know?

"Didn't I say 'scram' already?"

Jonah scrammed. Hopping on his bike, he pedalled down toward the shore. He was wrapped up tighter in this mess than a snail in its shell. He rushed to the bushes and puked.

"Oh…oh," he groaned, horrified.

He'd just barfed in Mr. Steevens' rowboat. The teacher was really gone! Long gone! And Jonah was an accomplice of sorts.

Oak Island loomed in the distance, its tree branches waving. He had to know whose hair he'd seen shining through the leaves that Saturday afternoon. He had to know before he could finally confess the truth—the whole truth, and nothing but the truth, so help him God.

The rowboat reeked of sour vomit as Jonah paddled against the tide. He hated the island now with its lure of treasure. With waves whipping against the boat, he gritted his teeth. Beaz should be here with him, helping him row.

Helping him think.

Finally reaching the shore, he beached the skiff. Jonah picked his way across the rocks and searched for the trail where they'd first come upon Mr. Steevens.

Blond hair glinted in the sun.

"Hello," he said. "Hello?"

The head of hair waved its tousled locks but no reply came. It was a woman…it had to be a woman. Who else did Mr. Steevens have squirrelled away on this island? Who did he leave stranded here?

Jonah shivered but boldly crept forward.

The hair remained steady, fluidly beckoning as he approached.

There was no body.

Just a long, thin, weathered pole.

The head of hair was simply a stringy mop, a remnant of times past. Perhaps from the recent days of the Texan oilmen, or even farther back when treasure hunters lived in the tiny Oak Island cabins. Like the one his father had said was attached to the back of Charlotte Barkhouse's home as her bedroom.

The chickens have come home to roost.

His great grandmother had said that a time or two. Everyone called her "Big Nanny" even though she was four foot eleven. And she was wise...if she were here, instead of tucked away in the convalescent home, she would see the irony of Charlotte's last breath being taken on this island. The place her tiny bedroom addition had once called home.

She might also scold him for the secrets he still harboured.

Following the matted path, Jonah soon came upon a clearing with a fire pit in the centre. The charred wood was cold and damp—no flames recently. Mr. Steevens was probably afraid of being discovered after Beaz had told him they had seen smoke. Jonah tried to remember what the teacher had said when he and Beaz had been stranded on the island.

Had he talked like he was—guilty?

Jonah had been so sure he'd seen Charlotte that day. But now he knew it had been a sun-bleached straggly mop, strewn over a tree branch and fluttering in the breeze.

Besides, the constable had confided to Jonah's father that Charlotte had been dead for days by the time the storm washed her up. And her clothing...she hadn't changed since the last day of school.

And Charlotte Barkhouse wouldn't be caught dead wearing the same thing two days in a row...

Cold shivers oozed up Jonah's spine. Did Mr. Steevens dump her body into the ocean after he'd dumped him and

Beaz onto the shore? Was he afraid of being discovered after they'd stumbled upon his hideout? Was Charlotte's dead body once in this very clearing, while the crazed teacher racked his brains for an escape?

He gulped. The locket! Had Mr. Steevens dumped Charlotte's lifeless body in the Money Pit?

But then how had she ended up behind the schoolhouse?

Staring at the holes where the tent pegs had left six indents, he wondered why Mr. Steevens had stuck around at all? *Why didn't he drive west and bury Charlotte's body in some farmer's field halfway across New Brunswick? He would have gotten off scot-free.*

The sun slipped behind a cloud.

Suddenly, Jonah felt very alone. He hadn't hidden the boat on the beach. Surely Mr. Steevens wouldn't find another way to come back to his island lair and do away with Jonah—a lone witness.

A paper fluttered across the clearing and Jonah stomped on it, catching the corner.

A map.

Of Oak Island.

With an "X" marked beside the word "treasure." Nowhere near the Money Pit.

Jonah crammed it into his pocket. The wind spoke as it rustled through the leaves; the word sounded like "run." He knew it was his imagination playing tricks on him again, just like it had with the blond-haired mop. If Beaz were here now, he'd be yammering about ghosts of long-dead pirates and treasure seekers. Jonah didn't believe in ghosts. But he did wonder why the sound in the trees seemed familiar.

Run! Run! Run!

Then he knew.

The lilting pitch sounded like Charlotte's voice.

CHAPTER 20

"LOOK UP ULCER," JONAH SAID.

Beaz flipped through the pages of the ancient medical book that he'd brought home from his grandmother's house in Halifax. "Brought on by stress. Symptoms are abdominal pain—"

"Got it," Jonah interjected.

"Vomiting."

"Did it."

"Blood in stool." Beaz grinned. "Hey, doesn't say anything about lockets."

"Quit the jokes. You haven't been here, Beaz," Jonah said. "You've missed the funeral, Sam Cooke's interrogation, skulking through the dark to mail that letter, finding the abandoned campsite on the island…you've got no idea how crazy things have been."

He didn't tell Beaz about his dad "owing" the constable—it sounded too ugly to repeat. Resentment grew in Jonah's chest. Beaz had left him in the thick of it, all alone. And after all, it was Beaz's hide Jonah had been protecting.

"Sorry," Beaz mumbled. He lifted his arm to scratch his ear and his shirtsleeve slid back revealing a black, purple, and blue circle.

"What happened to you?" The sharp pain gripped at Jonah's stomach again as he stared at the massive bruise.

"Nothing," Beaz said, yanking the sleeve back down to his elbow.

"Beaz?"

"I said nothing. Forget it."

"When's your mom coming home?"

"Don't know," Beaz mumbled. "Now the doctor thinks my grandmother doesn't have much longer." He sat stiffly on his kitchen chair, eyes not even seeming to focus on anything.

"Beaz?"

"Yeah?"

"I think we should throw the locket back in the Money Pit."

"Sure," Beaz said. "Like turning back time."

"Let's grab our gear." Jonah prayed Mr. Steevens' boat was still hidden in the bushes away from the prying eyes of the police. What if they had already been trampling over Oak Island in search of clues?

"We better get the locket first," Beaz said. "And I have three deliveries to make, including the Captain's dozen."

"Sam Cooke?" Jonah sputtered. "That crazy old man needs to get his own hens! That's the third time since Sunday he's wanted a dozen eggs."

"He's cracked!" Beaz grinned, his teeth popping out.

How does he do that? Jonah thought. *He smiles no matter what.*

After collecting the locket and the eggs, the boys went to the Wharf Prophet's driveway and stopped. The sound of mournful whistling drifted down the lane to where they paused beside the mailbox. "He'll ask me about the murder again," Jonah said. "I just know it."

"Maybe I should go by myself, then," Beaz offered.

"Sure," Jonah said. After all, the locket was jammed back in his pocket—Sam Cooke might smell it out somehow. Or hear its imaginary beat…

Beaz darted off and then returned in a flash. "Nothing," he said. "Gave him the eggs and he paid me without a word."

"Hmm," Jonah said.

"But…" Beaz paused, switching the basket of eggs to his other hand.

"What?"

"His hands were covered in blood again."

"He's nuttier than a fruitcake," Jonah said with a twinge of uncertainty. Crazy or not, Sam Cooke had an uncanny way of digging for the truth.

They meandered through Western Shore, delivering eggs. The final stop was the general store. Jonah scooped seven cents out of his pocket for a bottle of pop.

"Three cents short," Betty Schofield said, her bangles jangling as she counted the coins.

"But...but," Jonah stammered. Pop had gone up three cents in a week and a half.

"Supply and demand," Betty said smugly. "Can hardly keep it in stock now with all these tourists."

Jonah kicked at the gravel as he left without a pop. Betty was probably skipping in her spiky heels all the way to the bank every night. Charlotte's murder was the best thing to happen to Mrs. Schofield since her third husband had died the week after buying extra life insurance. Marvin Schofield had slipped and fallen down the stairs while Betty was on a buying trip in Halifax. It was ruled an accident—a very happy accident for Betty's bank account.

Thirsty, the boys returned to Jonah's to collect water and snacks for their final trip to the island. Jonah had already decided: row over, throw the locket in the Money Pit, row back. There would be no diversions.

Jonah's mom was lying on the sofa. "What are you boys up to now?" she croaked. She didn't look so good—her skin was yellow and her lips a sickly green colour.

"You okay, Mom?" Jonah stopped. "Where's Dad?"

"At his office in Mahone Bay." She licked her lips.

"Asiatic flu, I think. Just bring me a glass of water. I'll be fine."

"You sure?"

She waved her arm. "Off you go," she said, shutting her eyes.

And off they went, past the thriving general store and taking the familiar left down Crandall's Point Road. They were on a mission—a mission to turn back time.

At the end of the road, Jonah stopped.

Five police cars.

"Holy hillbilly!" Beaz gave a low whistle.

"It's over, Beaz." From the shore, Jonah could see the boats beached on Oak Island. "They know about the island. Now we gotta figure out something else to do with this stupid locket."

"At least our clue tipped them off," Beaz said hopefully, spinning his tires in the mud as he headed back up the hill.

As he pedalled home, Jonah wondered how simple decisions could grow so rapidly into tangled weeds.

"Jonah!" his father called out, when he pulled his bike into the driveway. "You need to come with me." Abraham Morgan's voice cut like cold steel. "Beaz, you'd better go home."

"Did something happen to Mom?" The pain twisted again in Jonah's stomach. Lately, he felt like he was always messing up. She'd looked really sick. He should have stayed with her.

"Mom's fine."

Dread sprouted in Jonah's chest. Even his arms tingled. "What happened?"

"They caught up with Marcus Steevens, as big as life, eating an ice cream cone in Chester. Crazy fool. Charged him with murder and now he wants me to represent him."

"Oh," Jonah said. "So what do you need me for?"

"That's what I'd like to know," his father snapped. "For some reason, that lunatic teacher wants to see me *and* you!"

"But not me?" Beaz whispered.

"Not you. But your mother called long distance from Halifax. She was looking for you."

Rocks pelted out behind Beaz's back wheel as he sped away without even saying goodbye.

Jonah didn't blame him for bailing. Beaz had his own demons to battle. Reaching into his pocket, he felt the cold, smooth metal of Charlotte's locket. There had been so many layers to the partial truth since that last day of school, Jonah wondered if he could even remember them all enough to keep them straight.

It likely didn't matter anymore. In a handful of moments he would be face to face with Mr. Steevens. The Oak Island secret was about to explode.

And there would be casualties.

But *not* Beaz, Jonah promised himself.

It was a vow he prayed he could keep.

Even if he had to lie.

CHAPTER 21

THE JAIL DIDN'T LOOK LIKE THE ONES IN western movies. There were no bars and bare mattresses. Instead, it was a cozy room with an extra lock and a high window. Not a very big window, but Jonah thought Mr. Steevens could possibly escape through it if he really put his mind to it. After all, there was a quilt-covered bed and a bureau—things that could be used in lieu of ropes and ladders.

There was also a basin of water and a slop bucket, but no toilet.

His dad explained on the way there that most people ended up in the "jail" to sleep off too much alcohol. It wasn't built for murderers, or long-term residents.

Jonah stared at the yellow walls while his dad met with the suspect in the constable's adjacent office. The whole place smelled like cabbage rolls with a twist of lemon. Really, the paint colour was too cheerful for a prison.

"We're ready for you," his dad said.

Examining his father's face, Jonah searched for any signs of things to come. What had Mr. Steevens divulged in the interview?

"I didn't kill her," Marcus Steevens said, tears welling in his eyes. "I would never hurt Charlotte."

Say nothing, Jonah thought. *Don't give anything away.*

Abraham Morgan cleared his throat. "Marcus thinks you can help clear him."

Jonah's mouth dropped open. Of all the things he had expected to hear, this was not one of them. Everything he knew about Charlotte's death pointed in the direction of the thin, scruffy half-kid, half-man staring him in the eye.

"You saw that I was alone on the island," Mr Steevens said. "Remember?"

"Umm…" Jonah broke off and stared at the floor.

"The day you were swimming and got caught in the tide."

Yanking his gaze back up, Jonah stared at his former teacher. What was he saying?

"Last Saturday, when I helped rescue you from the bay."

"You should have told me, son," his dad said. "First of all, your mother and I would have punished you if we'd known you swam out far enough to get caught in the current. Which, I suspect, is why you said nothing. But second, you knew the whereabouts of Marcus when the whole community was in an uproar. Why didn't you say anything after the storm? When Charlotte's body was found?"

"I…Beaz…me—"

"Beaz was still on the mainland," Mr. Steevens interrupted. "I heard Jonah yelling and helped him ashore. After he dried off, I rowed him back."

"Think, Jonah. Did you see any sign of Charlotte…ah, I mean her remains?"

He thought about the flowing hair of the dingy mop. "None," Jonah said.

"And what about Marcus? How did he seem? Was he nervous, excited?"

It was hard getting used to Mr. Steevens as "Marcus." A teacher's a teacher, not a person.

"He seemed okay. Friendly, I guess." Jonah watched Mr. Steevens' chest expand and settle, as if he'd finally sucked in a fresh gulp of air. Why had the teacher left the *Gingerale* and Beaz out of the Oak Island equation?

You keep my secret and I'll keep yours.

That's what Jonah had promised before Mr. Steevens had rowed them back to shore. Jonah shut his eyes. His former teacher was keeping up his end of the bargain—at least part of it. By omitting the boat, Mr. Steevens probably thought he'd be keeping Jonah and Beaz out of even bigger trouble. But why bother to lie about Beaz staying on the mainland? Wouldn't Beaz be another credible witness to the "normal" demeanour of a young schoolteacher just starting his summer holiday?

Mr. Steevens wanted Jonah on his side.

Badly.

Enough to lie. But why?

Does he know about Mrs. Hodder?

"I will consider taking your case," Abraham Morgan said thoughtfully. "But you must tell me the whole truth. I can't represent you properly if you don't. Understood?"

"Yes."

"Okay, let's review. You say you returned to your room at Betty Schofield's on the last day of school and packed up your belongings."

Mr. Steevens nodded.

"Why were you leaving so quickly?"

He shrugged. "It was the end of the month. I'd asked Betty if I could stay on a few extra days, but she said I'd have to pay rent for the whole month of July."

Jonah's dad gave a small smile. "That sounds like our dear Betty." He jotted a few notes. "And you gave Charlotte a drive home from school?"

Mr. Steevens crossed and uncrossed his legs. "You know I did."

"Yes," Jonah's dad said stiffly. "The police have a witness to her getting in your car, but no one recalls seeing her get out. Why did you take your car to school that morning?

It's not a long walk."

"I didn't. I walked to Betty's after dismissal and then brought my car back to pick up my teaching books. I intended to resign."

"Because?"

"Like I said, I was offered a job back in Ontario…with more pay."

"So you drove Charlotte home because she was upset?"

Jonah whipped his head up. Mr. Steevens' story now started to ring true—holding more details than even Jonah's eyewitness account.

"Yes," the teacher said. "She came back to the school and we…talked."

"And you're sure you don't know what was bothering her?"

"No."

Liar, Jonah thought.

"And why did you decide to go camping on Oak Island?"

After another leg cross and an "ahem" to clear his throat, Mr. Steevens said, "The treasure."

"Excuse me?"

Giving a feeble laugh, the teacher replied, "I wanted to try my hand at finding treasure on Oak Island. I found an old map folded in one of the textbooks at the school."

The map, Jonah thought. *There was a treasure map left behind at the campsite…*

Jonah's dad looked dubious. "Are you sure that's your answer to why you went there?"

Mr. Steevens' face burned bright red. "I thought if I had prospects of more money she might change her mind and come with me."

"Who?"

"Charlotte," he whispered.

CHAPTER 21

A FUNERAL ONE WEEK.

A carnival the next.

Such was life in the newly developing circus of Western Shore.

Ruth MacDonald had polled the residents on her daily tea visits and decided that Charlotte's former schoolmates needed a morale boost—and besides, the community should provide more entertainment for visitors now that their humble seaside village had hit the big time.

Jonah's mother speculated that Ruth's motives were more personal—Stan MacDonald had turned up dead drunk and stark naked in the graveyard the morning after Charlotte's funeral. "The poor woman needs to divert attention from Stan's inebriated escapades," she had murmured to his dad, not knowing that Jonah could hear them from the pantry, where he was foraging for gingersnaps.

His world was now officially spun upside down: his dad was defending his first murder suspect client, his mom was gossiping almost as much as Ruth MacDonald, and he...he was still withholding evidence.

In the shape of a golden heart.

He carried it with him always. It didn't seem safe to leave it anywhere—but he was afraid to have it in his pocket, too. What if the police searched him? The constable had scowled at him when they left the jail. What if he was arrested for not telling where Mr. Steevens was hiding?

Jonah would be heading back to Oak Island with his father and Constable Delray later that day, after the carnival. They wanted to clarify Jonah's testimony. This was his chance to help them and rid himself of guilt and gold. Maybe save his own skin.

He knew he'd have to somehow wander off and toss the locket back where it belonged—in the Money Pit.

At lunchtime, Jonah and Beaz trudged across the road to the carnival by the school. If anyone thought the location of the festivities was distasteful, they didn't speak of it. Children munched popcorn, cotton candy, and pretzels while Betty Schofield sold drinks by the dozen for ten cents a bottle. All the while, hundreds of people were standing within view of Charlotte's deathbed—of roses.

No one went close to them, though. The roses. There seemed to be an invisible line that none of the folks circling around the parking lot would cross.

Sam Cooke had his own table, selling pickled eggs and pickled herring.

"No wonder he lives alone," Jonah mumbled, remembering the Wharf Prophet's breath.

"Explains all those eggs he buys, though," Beaz added. "Pickles 'em."

"I guess so."

"Too bad Mom wasn't home to sell her bread here," Beaz said.

Jonah frowned, remembering Beaz's bruise. "When's she coming home?"

"After my grandmother dies." Beaz said it so matter-of-fact, like people died every day.

Jonah glanced at the rosebushes—maybe death was becoming more ordinary in Western Shore.

"Children, oh children! Over here," Ruth shouted. She beckoned everyone over to a grassy area near the back of the parking lot. Her husband stood close by, sipping a lemonade.

Beaz raised his eyebrows. "What's she got behind her back?"

"Candy for a scramble?" Jonah speculated.

"Free candy?" Beaz snorted. "Not with Betty Schofield running the canteen."

"Good point. I guess we'll know soon enough."

Ruth obviously wasn't about to announce her intentions

until everyone aged zero to twenty was plunked on the grass in front of her. She waited until even Marshall Delray, with his arms folded and a scowl on his face, stood near Jenny at the back of the gathering crowd.

Jonah's lip raised in half a smile as he nodded at Jenny. He couldn't seem to manage a full grin while standing at the scene of Mr. Steevens' inappropriate behaviour, Charlotte's murder, his own deceit, his father's...what?

Likely neither he nor Jenny nor half the dang crowd *wanted* to be here, but here they were—caught in the craziness of Ruth MacDonald's aspirations to be seen as something more than the butt of a joke.

Jenny nodded back, but didn't smile. Jonah wondered why she'd even come. The wounds from Charlotte's passing were fresh, open, yet the whole village was acting as if nothing was wrong. Even with Constable Deacon Delray patrolling through the crowds in his uniform, no one spoke a word about the deceased.

"Now, children," Ruth said. Her stiff smile exposed the gap between her two front teeth. "It's come to my attention that you all are feeling a little glum lately."

Percy Whalen, a grade one student, shrugged and his little sister, Peggy, scrunched up her nose, looking bewildered. A crowd of parents gathered, some of them frowning.

"Not everyone knows all the details, Ruth," Mrs. Whalen said cryptically.

"Nonsense," Ruth said. "Even little ones know *something* is going on."

Mrs. Whalen replied, "You'd better not give any details."

"What do you think I am, daft? I'm trying to lift their spirits, not drag everyone down in the dumps all over again."

A few parents chuckled at Ruth's rhetorical question. Jonah was sure they were all thinking the same thing: *Yes, you are daft.*

Whipping her arm out from behind her back, Ruth belted in a singsong voice, "Good afternoon tildren, I'n Ister Sockadoo."

One of Stan MacDonald's wool socks was tugged over Ruth's hand and down to her elbow. Cotton-ball eyes bobbed as she waved her arm around for the "puppet" show. Her words slurred as she clenched her teeth together and tried not to move her lips.

"Holy hillbilly," Beaz whispered. "She's cracked."

"*Completely* daft," Jonah agreed.

Older children and teens backed away from Ruth's one-woman show.

"Dun't ga…gaoo," she said. "I avf a storrry."

It was painfully long. Finally, Ruth gave up and had to move her lips so that "The Three Billy Goats Gruff" didn't come out sounding like "Da Tree Illy Goots Guff."

"It's like they've all forgotten Charlotte," Jonah said a few minutes later. Unconsciously, he reached into his pocket to check that the locket was still there—something he'd done a dozen times that day.

"I know," Beaz said, as they waited in line for the clothespin relay. "It sounds awful but I wish we could forget too."

It was Jonah's turn in the relay. He pinched the clothespin between his knees and waddled toward the narrow-necked empty milk bottle. The trick was to aim carefully and try to have the clothespin land inside.

He listened to the satisfying clink of the clothespin reaching its target. The watching crowd cheered, though some faces were still solemn—the faces of those most affected by Charlotte's passing.

Even Beaz cheered at the victorious clanking sound of their team winning.

Jonah tipped the bottle to retrieve the clothespin. He watched the object slide all the way out and still his brain didn't communicate what he was seeing until it had landed fully in his hand.

Charlotte's locket.

Glancing down, he saw the clothespin lying in the grass.

Jonah scanned the crowd as he closed his fingers over his palm. All eyes were watching.

But had they seen anything?

CHAPTER 22

"YOU'RE SURE YOU DIDN'T NOTICE?" JONAH ASKED again.

Shaking his head, Beaz said, "I'm telling you, all I heard was the sound. The bottle was sittin' in the taller grass. I don't think anyone saw the locket."

It was a hopeful thought, Jonah knew. A desperate longing, that when his biggest secret had been exposed, everyone else had been blind to it.

But was it realistic?

"Time to go," Abraham Morgan said, appearing at the doorway of Jonah's fort.

The three of them walked to the government wharf beside the schoolhouse. Jonah would officially be going to Oak Island. At the carnival, Jonah had begged for Beaz to be able to tag along and both fathers had agreed.

Constable Delray was waiting. "It's not a picnic," he barked, staring pointedly at Beaz.

"Settle down, Deacon," Jonah's dad said. "How often do

boys get permission to go to Oak Island? For goodness' sake, what harm can it do?"

"Stay out of trouble," the constable warned.

As the motor hummed, for the first time Jonah had an opportunity to take in the view as they clipped across the bay. He couldn't say he enjoyed it—that would be stretching the truth beyond imagination. His stomach still ached from the knowledge he concealed. Now he wondered if disposing of the locket would even bring peace. Had the opportunity for full disclosure come and gone and he'd missed it?

Yes, he admitted.

And now he was faced with the only other choice—throwing the locket away and pretending it had never been found.

He told himself it wouldn't have made any difference. Marcus Steevens killed Charlotte before anyone even knew she was missing. The teacher had been apprehended eating an ice cream cone—all had eventually been revealed. Nothing Jonah knew would have changed the outcome.

"I believe my client is innocent, Deacon. You should know that." Abraham Morgan stepped out of the boat onto Oak Island's shore.

Spit caught in Jonah's windpipe and he coughed repeatedly, unable to catch his breath.

"Even your son choked on that one," the constable said. "Could be you're gambling on the wrong horse. It wouldn't be the first time you've misplaced your trust."

"Not here!" Abraham Morgan hissed. "And I don't gamble. But if I did, I'd give odds a hundred to one that Marcus Steevens is innocent of murder."

"Just of the murder?" Constable Delray asked shrewdly.

"Why would he stay here for an extra week and then get a fill-up and an ice cream cone in Chester?"

"Two reasons," the constable said. "One, he didn't know she'd washed ashore. Two, he's a lunatic."

On the boat ride across the bay, Jonah had slipped the locket to Beaz. Now, as they stood on the beach waiting for directions, Jonah mumbled, "Is it okay if Beaz looks around a bit while I show you where I saw Mr. Steevens and his boat?"

"Don't care," the constable said, turning to Beaz. "But if you're not back in twenty minutes, you can swim home."

Beaz darted off and Jonah led his father and Constable Delray up toward the trees. "His boat was here," Jonah pointed. It felt good to speak the truth about something— Mr. Steevens *had* hidden his boat in this clump of brush. "And that's where I thought I saw Charlotte."

The mop seemed less alive now, the strands dull and shapeless. Jonah wondered how he'd ever mistaken it for Charlotte.

Wishful thinking.

"We've already scoured the island and found his campsite," the constable said, scratching his moustache. "No signs of a struggle."

"Good." Jonah's dad smiled. "I'll make sure I ask you about *that* on the witness stand."

"He had her lunch box. We found it near where his car had been parked."

Abraham Morgan chuckled. "The boy already admits to driving her home and to tossing her lunch box. So far his statement lines up with the evidence."

"Boy?" Constable Delray said. "He's a man at twenty-one. That girl was brutally murdered and he was her teacher! How can you even think of defending him? And why didn't your own son tell the truth about seeing him? Seems you have trouble keeping the reins on both of your kids."

"Keep quiet, Jonah," his dad said, his voice steely. "I'll answer that. He didn't know the teacher was suspected of murder at the time."

Jonah squirmed. This time it had nothing to do with his own guilt. Why did the constable keep referring to him *and* his brother?

"What about later?" Constable Delray quipped.

"Nothing has been proven, Deacon," Abraham Morgan said, looking the officer squarely in the eye. "We all have our own secrets to carry. It's best you remember that. Keep your focus on the case. What about that note? Have you figured out who sent it?"

Jonah's heart thudded. What were they saying? What secrets? How did they know about the note? Did Marshall tell his brother about the note?

"What difference does it make?"

"Why didn't the person who found the car just call the police? Why did they have to hide their identity?"

Wrong note, Jonah thought. They weren't talking about Marshall's note. They were discussing *his* anonymous note that he mailed to the police—the one revealing the location of Mr. Steevens' hidden car. Should he confess? Maybe it would keep him out of trouble if they knew he really had tried to tell the police about the teacher's whereabouts.

Constable Delray shrugged. "Some people don't like to fuss with the police. I'm sure it's nothing out of the ordinary."

"Well, I'm not," Abraham Morgan said. "As a matter of fact, I think whoever sent that note could very well be an alternate suspect."

Jonah's knees buckled and he sat down on a seaweed-covered rock. The dried plant pods crackled under his weight. What was his father saying?

Beaz stumbled along the beach, breathlessly yelling, "I'm back! Don't leave without me!"

Climbing into the boat, Beaz slid into the seat next to Jonah. "It's done," he whispered. And he was smiling—the relief seemed to make his pearly white teeth glow brighter in the setting sunlight.

Jonah wondered if he had the heart to give the latest round of disastrous news to Beaz. His best friend looked as if the weight of the world had been lifted off his shoulders. "Tell me what you did with it," he whispered back.

"I dropped the locket onto one of the beams. Not one as far down as before. One near the top. One I could reach without a rope."

Jonah nodded. "So someone can still find it?"

"Yup."

"Good," Jonah said, licking his sandpapery lips. "Beaz?"

"Yup?"

Jonah swallowed hard. He didn't need to worry about being overheard, the sound of the motor drowned out their whispering. Besides, his dad and the constable were arguing heatedly over the case. Now that Abraham Morgan was counsel for the defence, the officer no longer seemed to value the lawyer's opinions about Charlotte's death.

"I've got bad news," Jonah said.

Beaz's face drained of colour. "What now?"

"My dad thinks I'm the murderer."

CHAPTER 24

"There was something not quite right about that man when he first came here," Ruth MacDonald said. "He nearly ruined the entire carnival selling those nasty pickled eggs."

"Only because Betty couldn't sell her rubbery stale ones. Sam Cooke should go into business." Jonah's mother sighed.

He couldn't see them from the dining room where he was reading his father's notes while pretending to pore over orange puzzle pieces that were part of the Grand Canyon. It's funny how adults forgot children were around—especially if the children kept quiet. Jonah held his breath, not wanting to spoil the chance to hear Ruth's new tidbit about Sam Cooke.

"Besides," Jonah's mother added, "he's been here for ten years, Ruth, and has been nothing but kind."

"No one ever shows up to visit—no family, anyway, and he wears that wire-thin wedding band and never speaks of a wife, past or present. What happened to her? That's what I'd like to know."

"Your Stan doesn't wear his ring, does he?"

Ruth slammed down her china cup. "Thank you for the tea, Muriel. I'll be on my way."

The kitchen door squeaked open and banged shut.

"Come sit down and have a snack, Jonah." His mother sighed again.

He gave a final glance at his father's chart lying beside the puzzle and poked his head through the doorway. "Didn't think you knew I was there."

"Really?" she said, raising her eyebrows. "You'd be surprised what I know."

Squirming under her scrutiny, he bit into a soft, flaky tea biscuit smeared in marmalade. He chewed appreciatively and gulped a mouthful of milk. "Why do you bother to have her in for tea?"

Now it was his mother's turn to fidget under his gaze. "She knocks on my door. I can't very well leave her standing outside while I duck behind the curtain."

Jonah stared at his mom like he was seeing her for the very first time.

She brushed a strand of hair from her face. "It's not very Christian of me, is it? I used to think that it was, smiling no matter what and brewing a fresh pot of tea for that woman. But now I can hardly keep a civil tongue around Ruth MacDonald, God bless her spiteful, tiny heart."

His mom was like that—shining light on things that other adults pretended weren't so. But lately she seemed to have even less patience for facades.

"Aren't you afraid you'll...you know," Jonah stopped. He couldn't think of how to word it. How did you ask your mother if she was afraid of making a mistake so big that it might have a fiery consequence? "Go to hell," he finally sputtered. "Aren't you afraid of that?"

"Is everything okay, Jonah?" She wrapped her arm around his shoulder. "You seem more...moody lately. You and I are a right cranky pair."

He shrugged her hand away. "What about it, Mom?"

"God knows I'm not perfect and so do you and your father. I try not to be uncharitable, but when I make mistakes, as I often do, I ask for forgiveness."

Setting his plate and glass in the sink, he said, "Beaz and I are going for a bike ride. Maybe up to see the new school in Gold River."

"It's not difficult, Jonah."

"What?"

"To ask for forgiveness." She twisted the stopper into the sink and turned on the faucet. White foaming soap bubbles inched across the soiled dishes.

"Sure," he said, racing out the door and hopping on his

bike. He wondered if some mistakes were harder for God to forgive than others.

Maybe.

Beaz was waiting at the bottom of his driveway, so Jonah whizzed by without stopping. The wind whipped through his hair and he pedalled ferociously until his foot slipped and his ankle scraped against the jagged metal.

"Dang!" He bit his lip but resisted the urge to jam on his brakes until he spun into the parking lot of the new Gold River–Western Shore Consolidated School. A crew of painters were coating the wooden siding with a bright white.

"It's bleeding," Beaz said, panting. "You were pedalling like your pants were on fire."

"Trying to shake off trouble," Jonah said, wiping the blood from his ankle. "Somehow it always catches up with me."

"Does your dad still think Mr. Steevens is innocent?"

Nodding, Jonah said, "He's got a whole chart. A timeline, he calls it. He works on it every night on the dining room table. I even dragged out my stupid Grand Canyon puzzle so I can keep an eye on things. He's got a big question mark, circled in red pencil, by the words 'anonymous note.'"

"Holy hillbilly." Beaz rubbed his eye. "You gotta tell him. Everything, before it's too late."

"I can't," Jonah said. He was afraid if he opened up the whole treasure-hunting can of worms, Beaz would be black and blue from head to toe. Besides, he wasn't a hundred percent sure his own hide wouldn't get a good tanning.

Maybe he could quietly beg for forgiveness. No one else needed to know. Did God stuff work like that?

"What about the locket?" Beaz asked. "Did Mr. Steevens give it to her?"

"That's part of my own puzzle I'm trying to work out, Beaz. Dad doesn't seem to care too much about that. Must be because he didn't actually *see* the locket."

"Or swallow it." For once Beaz said it like it wasn't funny.

"Nope." Jonah scratched at a mosquito bite on his forehead. He was a fine mess—a mosquito-bitten, ankle-bleeding coward. "Mr. Steevens admits he gave her the locket."

"I knew it!" Beaz's eyes widened. "He killed her, Jonah, he really did."

"There's more." Biting his lip, Jonah wondered why it mattered. But deep down in the pit of his stomach he knew it did. "Mr. Steevens gave her the locket, but insists that according to the evidence, it wasn't the murder weapon."

"Yeah, right."

Rev. Lowe, one of the painters, turned and raised his

cap to the boys. Jonah waved back absentmindedly at his favourite storyteller. Rev. Lowe painted during the week and preached on Sundays—as an itinerant minister, he'd travelled around Nova Scotia since he was nineteen and had collected an imaginary trunk full of amusing tales.

"She was strangled by the chain." The words tumbled from Jonah's mouth like raindrops pounding on a tin roof.

"What's the difference?"

"Mr. Steevens said he couldn't afford a chain but he gave her the locket anyway."

"So where did…how did?"

"I guess he doesn't know." Jonah watched Rev. Lowe's brush whisk across the wood siding without spilling a drop of paint. "He says he gave her the locket on St. Valentine's Day, but that the last day of school was the first time she wore it. He says he was shocked to see it."

"On a chain he didn't give her," Beaz whispered.

"The chain that killed her." Jonah's heart thudded. It seemed like a small thing, an insignificant detail. It reminded him of something he couldn't quite bring into focus.

"So where's the chain now?"

"Don't know," Jonah shrugged. "Never thought about *that*. I guess it must be in the Money Pit. It must have fallen down further than the locket."

Smiling, Beaz sighed. "So really, we didn't keep the whereabouts of the murder weapon a secret. We have no idea where the chain is."

"I guess," Jonah said, knowing they had twisted the truth and half-truths like a red-and-white barber's pole—ordered and fluid. But underneath something nagged at him. Because as much as a barber's pole twirled like there was no beginning or end to the pattern...there was.

It was simply a way to trick the mind.

An illusion...

CHAPTER 25

It was the hottest day in fifty-three years according to Western Shore's unofficial weatherman, Charlie Rankin. Sam Cooke might forecast unusual signs and wonders, but Charlie kept official data—stacks of Hilroy notebooks with temperature and barometer readings. Four times a day for the last sixty-six years he had measured and recorded his findings.

"It's a heat wave," Betty Schofield said needlessly, fanning herself with a stack of dollar bills from her cash register.

Jonah scooped the last bottle of pop from the cooler and counted out five pennies to add to the nickel he'd placed on the counter.

"Want an ice cream cone to go with that? Half price." She whipped the bills faster in front of her face as if offering any kind of a deal might give her heart palpitations and send her to an early grave. "Can't keep the darn stuff cold enough in this heat."

"No, thank you," Jonah said, grateful she hadn't made up for her loss on the ice cream by charging an extra nickel for the last chilled pop. He scooted out of the store before she could read his mind and up the price.

The fizzy cold sweetness slid down his throat.

"Hey, kid."

A bubble of extra air pushed its way down with the pop and Jonah hiccupped. "Hey," he said, trying to decide where to look. The ground? The tree? Marshall's face? That was the thing about keeping secrets and telling half-truths—you felt like they were written in your eyes for anyone to read.

But can Marshall Delray read?

It was a mean, spiteful thought. Not very Christian, as his mother would say. After all, one of the biggest secrets Jonah was keeping was Marshall's note. If the big ape could write it, then it was a given he could read it.

"You're off the hook," Marshall said. The older boy's dark eyes held nothing to be deciphered. "My brother knows about my note."

"The constable? How? What?"

"He found it in that crazy teacher's car. Recognized my handwriting."

"So why are you telling me?" Jonah ventured. After blurting it out he realized that even by asking, he wasn't showing Marshall proper respect for his esteemed position—Western Shore chief bully.

"Because I kept *you* out of it."

"Oh...but..." Jonah watched Marshall's Adam's apple bounce while he swallowed. His neck resembled an overgrown tree trunk. "Why?" Jonah finally managed to croak through dry lips before he took another gulp of pop.

Marshall shrugged. "Did you a favour. You owe me. Also didn't rat you out for going to the island. I guess you owe me twice."

Choking on his drink, Jonah felt the burn of liquid sliding up through his nostrils. Owing Marshall Delray anything sounded almost as appealing as getting his tongue stuck to frosty metal in January—painful and awkward. And it reminded him of the constable's words to his father: "You owe me..."

"The island?" Stumbling over the words, Jonah tried his best to sound incredulous. "Your bro...Constable Delray knows I was there after being rescued by Mr. Steevens. And I went back there yesterday on the police boat."

"Sure." Marshall grinned. "But you and I know those weren't the only times you were there."

"I..."

"Saw you," Marshall interjected. "Diggin' in the Money Pit. Know you found something, too."

It must be like drowning, that feeling of not being able to breathe while the stellar moments of your life flash by on a movie screen inside your brain. That's how Jonah felt now, smothered and desperate for a simpler time—a time when he hadn't been too busy covering up his own deceit to shed light on other life-and-death secrets.

What about Beaz? Did Marshall see him, too?

"Even know what day it was," Marshall continued. "Same day Deacon came home mad as a hatter about the teacher's car disappearing before he got to it."

I was alone on the island that day, Jonah thought, relief seeping through him. Beaz was protected.

"Didn't know I was there, did ya?" Marshall spit into the dirt. "Kept an eye on you the whole time, saw you dig something gold out of the Money Pit. What was it, anyway? A charm? A locket, maybe?"

But I didn't go to the Money Pit that day…

"Yeah, a locket," Jonah said, his heart pounding. *How does Marshall know about the locket?* He'd obviously made up the part about seeing Jonah at the Money Pit. Maybe he'd seen Jonah rowing over, but he hadn't followed. If he had, he'd know about the map at Mr. Steevens' campsite, not the locket. Wrong day, wrong time, wrong clue.

Internally, Jonah groaned. The map. He'd forgotten to give it to his dad. Well, maybe not *forgotten* as much as *neglected*. After all, it helped bring credibility to the teacher's story and at the time, Jonah had known his father's client was guilty.

Innocent until proven otherwise. That's what his father had said at the very first community meeting after Charlotte had disappeared.

How did Marshall *really* learn about the locket? He'd been behind him at the carnival, the next in line for the clothespin relay. Was that when he saw it?

"So you must have noticed the locket when it landed in the milk jug," Jonah said. "At the carnival?"

"Sure," Marshall said. "I had a hard time not laughing my head off. You with your secret pirate's treasure out in the open for everyone to see."

Pirate's treasure.

Blinking his eyes shut and holding them closed for a moment, Jonah's thoughts trickled to the puzzle pieces lying on his dining room table: the vibrant orange, the burnt red, one piece often resembling another—almost interlocking, but not quite the right fit.

Marshall knew Jonah had the locket. That was easily explained by the mishap at the carnival. But Marshall lied about seeing Jonah at the Money Pit, so how did he *really* know that the locket had been found there?

Jonah opened his eyes and stared again at Marshall's neck.

Click.

A piece of the puzzle slid into place.

"So where is it?" Marshall asked. "The locket?" His eyes flashed, anger written clearly now.

Shrugging, Jonah said, "Threw it back, it was jinxed."

Marshall unconsciously fingered the links of the gold chain around his neck. "Jinxed," he echoed. "Maybe all pirate's gold carries a curse."

"Maybe," Jonah agreed. "Um, well…I gotta go meet Beaz now. We've got plans."

It was a lie.

Walking away, Jonah expected to feel a hand clamp down on his shoulder. Marshall was stupid, really stupid. But was he too stupid to realize that Jonah now knew the truth?

CHAPTER 26

JONAH POUNDED ON BEAZ'S FRONT DOOR. "COME on, Beaz, where've you been all day? I have to talk to you!"

The door swung open. "Beasley isn't available," Mrs. Hodder said icily.

"Oh," Jonah sputtered. "You…home…early."

"Good thing I am," she replied. "The whole place has gone to hell in a hand basket. The coop's a mess, deliveries forgotten, clothing missing…" her voice trailed off and she scowled, like she was perturbed she'd run out of things to list.

Jonah hung his head. "I guess I didn't clean the coop very well last week."

"Nonsense! Beasley's been back from Halifax long enough to clean up your mess and more. Now, if you'll excuse me, I have to give *that woman* a cup of tea." She slammed the door shut.

Now what?

Pacing to the end of the wharf and back, Jonah felt like his head was going to explode as he mentally rearranged the puzzle of Charlotte's murder. Pieces had been forced too soon and assumptions had been made incorrectly—yet even now, he was ending up with edge pieces in the middle and fragments of the ground mixed with the sky.

He stared at Charlotte's deathbed from the opposite direction, down on the wharf. Wild roses bloomed in their fuchsia glory, peeking over the seawall standing guard behind the one-room schoolhouse. Years ago, volunteers had constructed an unusually high rock barrier to protect the treasured building from being ravaged by an angry ocean.

"Hot as Hades," the Wharf Prophet said.

Jonah jumped. Sam Cooke had sidled up beside him without making a sound.

"The waves didn't go over the wall during the storm, did they?"

"Not here," Sam pointed. "Further down."

"So she was there under the rosebushes the whole time."

"What made you think she wasn't?"

"Thought she washed in from Oak Island." Once the words were out, Jonah knew he couldn't bring them back. "I mean later…I thought that later, not at first," he stammered, knowing that of all people in Western Shore, the Wharf Prophet would decipher the truth lurking in Jonah's eyes.

"People see me without really paying attention," Sam Cooke said. "After a while, I become a part of the landscape."

An uneasy feeling took root in Jonah. "Did you see what happened to Charlotte?"

"Heavens, no! Do you think I would let that poor family suffer like this, if I could prove what happened to that girl?"

Prove. He said prove, not know.

"Why were your hands covered in blood when we delivered your eggs?" Jonah said boldly, meeting the Wharf Prophet's own eyes to see what they revealed.

Sorrow, blended with—amusement.

"Paint," Sam Cooke said. "Red paint, not blood. My wife, Bonnie, always used to say I was as sloppy as the day is long. She died twelve years ago. Some days I miss her something fierce."

For ten years, the gossips of Western Shore had waited for a whisper from Sam Cooke about his life before settling here, and the old fisherman had given them nothing. But to Jonah he'd mentioned a wife—probably the person who'd lovingly hooked the rugs and collected the mismatched china in the Wharf Prophet's kitchen. Sloppy or not, Sam Cooke had kept his wife's memory alive by keeping the kitchen spotless.

Now Jonah, who had been given a glimpse beyond the wild hair and pickled eggs, inwardly refused to pry any further.

Instead, he said, "Marshall killed Charlotte." The words fell out easily, as if he'd said something benign like "It might rain," or "Pass the salt."

"Can you prove it?" Sam Cooke said eagerly, and some of the hard lines from years of weathering both storms and sun slipped away from the old man's face.

"I don't know," Jonah replied. "I'm going to talk to my dad. I think I have a lot of explaining to do."

Explaining the mystery, while still keeping old secrets.

"Sounds like most fourteen-year-old boys," the Wharf Prophet chuckled. He strode away, whistling a tune Jonah didn't recognize.

Crossing the road, Jonah felt as though he was finally doing something right in all this mess. Maybe his new clues would help free an innocent man. As he drew closer to home, the weights that had started to make permanent dents in his shoulders lifted.

"Hi, Mom," he said.

She was facing the wall, telephone receiver in her hand. Not moving. Not hearing.

"Mom?"

Turning around, her face was pale and eyes wet. "Sit down," she mumbled.

"What is it? Are you okay? Is Dad okay? Big Nanny?"

"There's been a terrible accident," she said slowly, repeatedly patting the back of his hand.

"What happened?" He yanked his hand away. "Mom!"

"It's Beaz," she said. "He fell down the stairs and…hit his head. It's serious."

No!

There were no jokes to be made, no wisecracks to soften the news. No toothy grin from Beaz as he compared his own fate to one of Betty's gaggle of husbands.

"Where is he? I was just at his house!" Jonah shouted, but the words didn't seem to make sense as he spoke them aloud. "I need to see him!"

"Your father and Mr. Hodder are taking him to Dawson Memorial in Bridgewater."

Jonah grabbed her arm. "You have to take me there, please."

The seconds ticked slower than last summer's road trip to Saint Andrews, New Brunswick. But really, the hospital was only about twenty-five minutes away. Jonah's head knew this, but his heart counted the time differently…in hateful slow motion.

Beaz might die, he thought, and then he pushed the words away.

"How did it happen?" Jonah asked.

His mother said nothing.

"She did it, didn't she? His mother?" His breathing was jagged now and his words cut the air. It was past time for this secret to be exposed. Mrs. Hodder was home and Beaz was near dead.

It was past time for pretending.

"Now, Jonah—"

"He hides it," Jonah said, blinking back tears. If he gave into them, they'd gush and never stop. "She beats him and he smiles like a stupid monkey at the circus."

"Jonah! Don't call him that. He's your friend!"

Groaning, Jonah pulled his knees up to his chest. "It's too late," he said. "It's all too late. I should have told you about the bruises."

"You're a boy," his mother said. "It's not up to you to fix what's wrong in grown-ups' brains. That woman isn't right in the head. We all knew it, but no one did anything until it was too late."

Her words sucked him back from his private hell. Back to daylight. "Too late? Is he—"

"I meant before something serious happened," she hurried to explain. "Sit back, Jonah, we'll know about Beaz soon enough."

As she pulled into the hospital parking lot, Jonah flung open the car door and ran into the waiting area. "Dad!" he cried, falling into his father's arms.

"It'll be okay, son," Abraham Morgan said, smoothing Jonah's tousled hair.

"I should've told," Jonah sobbed. "I'm sorry! I should've told you everything."

CHAPTER 27

HE TRIED NOT TO SLEEP. TWISTING HIS BODY to stave off comfort, Jonah eyed the mute electric clock on the waiting room wall. It seemed disloyal that he should have one ounce of ease while the doctor worked through the night to stop Beaz's hemorrhaging.

Finally, the first rays of dawn spilled into the waiting room.

"Jonah," Mr. Hodder whispered, shaking him gently.

"What is it?" Had he been sleeping?

"Beaz is in recovery."

It's nice he calls him Beaz, Jonah thought before asking, "Is he…okay?"

"For now," Mr. Hodder said, cupping his face in his hands as his shoulders began to shake. "I didn't know," he sobbed. "Not how bad she really was."

"Dad," Jonah whispered, poking his father. "Dad, Mr. Hodder needs you to…talk to him for a bit."

Abraham Morgan stirred and stretched. "Let's find

some coffee," he said, resting his hand on Mr. Hodder's shoulder as they walked away.

Jonah watched them leave, thinking that one day he and Beaz might be fathers going for coffee—if Beaz lived. "Mom?" Jonah whispered.

"What, honey?"

"Where's Mrs. Hodder?"

"That's a hard question, Jonah."

"A hard question or a hard answer?"

She flashed a half-smile. "You're not really a kid anymore, are you?"

It seemed rhetorical, so he waited silently for her to decide on how to tackle his question.

"She's going into the hospital for a bit," she finally said.

"Here?" Jonah asked. His heart pounded. Would Beaz be safe with his mother lurking around?

Muriel Morgan shook her head. "In Halifax," she whispered, glancing around the empty room. "At the N. S., for observation."

The N.S. The mental hospital. Jonah sighed. At least Beaz was out of harm's way for now. "What about when she's out?"

"Beaz will be protected, Jonah," his mother said firmly. "I give you my word that she will not be allowed to lay a hand on that boy again." Her face held the air of a ferocious mother bear.

Protective.

Jonah felt the muscles in his chest relax. His mother would help him look after Beaz—he wasn't fighting shadows of Mrs. Hodder single-handedly anymore. With a guilty twinge, he realized he never should have tried to wage this battle alone.

Or any other battle.

"I'm going to find Dad," he said.

His shoes made a gentle squashing noise against the tile—the hospital was slow to wake and no other sounds competed with his solitary walk. Following the wafting scent of eggs, toast, and coffee, he planned his words.

"Have a seat, son," his dad said. He and Mr. Hodder were sipping tiny cups of coffee in a small alcove.

"I should go back to Beaz now," Mr. Hodder said.

Alone with his father, Jonah couldn't remember any of the words he'd rehearsed. "I kept stuff from you to keep me and especially Beaz out of trouble," he blurted. The words tumbled out, not really even making sense.

"I see." Abraham Morgan folded and unfolded his arms.

"It was nothing that would have changed anything. Not for Charlotte. It started with the note."

"What note?"

"The first one. You must know about it by now. The constable does. He found it in the car."

Abraham Morgan shook his head. "I know about the

anonymous note mailed to the police, but that's not what you're talking about, is it?"

Taking a deep breath, Jonah started his story—one that included all of the murky parts, all of the weeds, and all of the puzzle pieces he had accumulated up until now.

"Don't you see, Dad?" he said finally. "Marshall has to be the one who killed Charlotte."

"Marshall gave her the chain? How do you know?"

"I'm guessing. Jenny said that Charlotte used to like Marshall. It must have driven him crazy to see Mr. Steevens' locket on *his* chain. When he gave me the note that afternoon, his shirt was all mussed but he wasn't wearing that chain, I'm sure of it. He must have roughed her up and she ran into the schoolhouse."

"Marcus Steevens swears that nothing *ever* happened between him and Charlotte. Of course he would deny it if it did, but oddly enough I believed him. He says she was upset at the schoolhouse that time you saw them together, but she wouldn't tell him what was wrong. If she *was* attacked by Marshall after school, that would explain her clothing…"

"I bet Marshall caught up with her again later. But this time he went too far. You were right, Dad. Mr. Steevens *is* innocent."

"We're guessing, Jonah. There's really no proof."

"Marshall knew where I found the locket. He must have thrown it in the Money Pit himself after killing Charlotte. And what about the note in Mr. Steevens' car? Constable Delray has to show *that* to you now."

Draining his coffee cup, Abraham Morgan stared past Jonah. "You'd do anything for Beaz, wouldn't you?"

"Of course, why would you even ask me that?"

"Beaz is your friend, not your brother."

"Yeah, but—" Jonah broke off, understanding. Deacon Delray hadn't mentioned the note in the investigation. "He wouldn't destroy it, would he? To protect Marshall?"

His dad gave a wry smile. "Until lately, I'd have bet my life you were the most honest boy I knew…but look what you kept hidden to protect Beaz. I don't know if Deacon will uphold justice at the expense of his brother."

A reputation crumbled. More than one, really: Jonah's, Mr. Steevens', Mrs. Hodder's, Constable Delray's… "Why do you say that? Even Mom says Deacon Delray is good at his job."

Abraham Morgan tugged at his sleeve. "Sitting in this hospital brings back a flood of memories, son. There are things we do for our loved ones. Things that seem right at the time."

"What are you saying, Dad?" Jonah remembered that Caleb had been pronounced dead in this very hospital. Not even his parents had been permitted to see the body.

The "closed" casket had been laid to rest in the family plot in Martin's Point. There had been no closure for the family. Not visually, at least. Just the vacancies—Caleb's room, his seat at mealtime, his car gone from the driveway…

"I don't know if Deacon would do the right thing because I can't say that I would."

"You would tell," Jonah insisted, his heart pounding.

"I've been keeping a secret to protect someone, too," his dad said.

There were no secrets left, were there? Jonah reviewed everything he'd just told his father. "I told you everything. I'm sure of it."

Abraham Morgan shook his head. "Not you, your brother. He was driving drunk the night he crashed. Only the constable and I knew that at the time. Since no one else's property was damaged, Deacon agreed to keep it quiet."

Another reputation crumbled. Two, really: his brother, his father.

"Why are you telling me now?" Jonah whispered.

"No one's perfect, Jonah. Not you, not me, not your brother."

The dull ache left in his stomach surprised him—the moment of his brother's unmasking left him feeling empty. There was no joy in this truth. Just truth. "Does Mom know?"

"She guessed a few months after the accident. In a strange way, knowing helped her heal. Let's go check on her now. She's probably nauseous again. Not a very comfortable rest for her last night."

"She's still sick?" Jonah asked. "I thought she was over the flu."

Slapping Jonah lightly on the shoulder, his dad said, "Not sick, expecting. Next January you're going to be the big brother. We've been keeping the news quiet until the doctor confirmed what we already suspected."

A new life. So maybe all secrets weren't bad.

Reading materials in hospitals were so notoriously ancient they could have been chiselled on stone tablets. At least that's what Jonah's mother announced when they returned to the waiting room. She shuffled through the array of dog-eared magazines missing their covers and hard-covered Bible storybooks with their pages frayed.

"I told him the news," Abraham Morgan said. "About the baby."

Jonah sat down awkwardly beside his mother, not sure what to say. "Congratulations, I guess."

"Thank you, I guess." She smiled.

He stared at a decrepit issue of *The Saturday Evening Post* lying open on the top of the pile. 1939. He didn't stop to wonder how an almost twenty-year-old magazine survived the journey to end up at the Dawson Memorial.

Instead, he stared at the familiar words blaring from the page: "The Money Pit."

Driving away from the hospital later that morning, Jonah tried to shut off thinking about Beaz by stewing over Oak Island. The article had swirled with theories, all rustlings that had whispered their way through Western Shore during Jonah's lifetime: Captain Kidd, the Spaniards, the French. Thinking about the money that had been poured into treasure hunting on the island, Jonah knew that the Money Pit had earned its name a thousand times over.

The lure of treasure had consumed so many: Caleb, Marshall, Mr. Steevens, him and Beaz. What good was a thirst for money if at the end of the day Marshall was a killer, Mr. Steevens was in jail, and Beaz was—what? Stable?

What about Charlotte? She'd actually worn Marshall's Oak Island treasure around her neck and *not* lived to tell about it. Would things get worse for all of Western Shore if the treasure was found? "I'm going to Oak Island this afternoon," Jonah said.

His mother sat frozen, saying nothing. Jonah braced himself for her inevitable protest.

"Why? And how will you get there?" his father asked. "You've got no boat."

"Sam Cooke will take me, don't worry. There's

something I really need to do. Please, Mom? Dad?" He held his breath.

"Muriel?"

"As long as an adult goes with him," his mother said.

"I promise I won't go alone." Jonah leaned back in the seat and closed his eyes.

CHAPTER 28

HE MEANT TO TURN OFF AT VAUGHN ROAD, BUT it seemed as if the wheels of his bike had a mind of their own. The headstone was in place, but the grass had yet to sprout. Charlotte Evelyn Barkhouse was a buried treasure in her own right.

Silence blanketed the graveyard—there was no telltale knock of the woodpecker today. Jonah's own heartbeat had quieted as well. He couldn't have saved Caleb or Charlotte, but he might have been able to save Beaz. It was an ugly truth and he stared it in the face.

"Hey, kid, what are you doing here?"

The voice sent chills down Jonah's back. "It's a free country," he answered, spinning around and staring at Charlotte's killer.

Marshall's eyes were red. Jonah wasn't expecting that.

"She was really beautiful," Marshall whispered, looking surprisingly like a human being. "I can't believe she's dead."

Jonah wasn't expecting *that*, either. Taking in Marshall's broad shoulders and overgrown biceps, Jonah knew that he had to fight with his wits. Possibly he could save another innocent person—Mr. Steevens. "Beaz is in the hospital," he said.

"I heard already. Ruth MacDonald hasn't shut up about it since yesterday."

"Has she bothered to mention that her flapping gums are what put Beaz there in the first place?"

"What are you talking about?"

The full force of anger hadn't smacked Jonah until that moment. "She was waiting for us when we got back from the hospital. Decided it was her duty to tell my parents that I had gone to Oak Island with Beaz in the *Gingerale*—the same thing she told Mrs. Hodder yesterday before Beaz took a flying leap down the stairs."

"Witch." Marshall slapped at a hornet.

Deep down, Jonah knew the anger for Ruth was really just a disguise for how he felt about himself. He could have protected Beaz from the beginning. "You were right, Marshall, that island is cursed." He swallowed, about to garner the last bit of proof. "Can't believe you and I both went there this summer."

Marshall's cheeks flared in crimson splotches. "I didn't. Haven't stepped foot on the place since I went with Caleb two years ago."

Liar.

"I need a way over there. Today." Jonah heard his own breathing and somehow it let him know that this wasn't a nightmare. It was reality.

"You're crazy," Marshall snarled. "You just said the place was cursed and now you want to go back. What for?"

"There's something I need to do. For Beaz." Jonah waited. When he'd told his parents that he was going back to the island, he'd thought the Wharf Prophet would take him over. But this was better. Once he found out where Marshall's boat was stashed, maybe there would be proof of what had happened to Charlotte at the big ape's grimy hands. He knew Marshall was lying about being on the island this summer—he just needed evidence to make something right in all of this mess.

Fingering the chain around his neck, Marshall nodded. "Meet me at the government wharf in thirty minutes."

Jonah's stomach gurgled like he'd feasted on another bottle of prunes. Why would Marshall risk setting out for Oak Island from the government wharf? At the same time, it brought him an element of peace—there would be witnesses before he set out for the cursed island with a crazed killer. That might increase his chances of coming back alive.

Thirty minutes later, Jonah arrived at the government wharf and found the police boat chugging a haphazard welcome. Marshall and his brother waited on deck. "Deacon said he'd take us over."

Interrupting Jonah's open-mouthed surprise, Sam Cooke strolled over, winding in his reel. "Out for a cruise, gentlemen?" the fisherman asked.

Deacon smirked. "Marshall and Jonah twisted my arm. Seems both of them want to say a final goodbye to all those millions before they decide to grow up and do some real work for a living."

"Don't mind if I do," the Wharf Prophet said, jumping onto the deck of the boat as if he'd been invited.

They were an odd group, bouncing across the waves. For once, Jonah hoped that all of the spyglasses of Western Shore were trained on them. He wanted witnesses.

"I want to go to the Money Pit," Marshall said, turning to Jonah. "What about you?"

"Doesn't matter."

The police boat raced toward the island's shore and just like the first time he'd set foot on the island, Jonah heard the leaves whispering unintelligible warnings. Goosebumps covered his arms and he tried to warm himself.

"Lonely place," Sam Cooke said. "Haven't been here for a bit, myself."

Jonah had brought a knapsack with him and slung it over his shoulder as he stepped into the water and sloshed ashore.

"What's in there?" Deacon Delray asked.

"Coal shovel, water, couple cookies. No big deal." He'd omitted something from the list and there still was a slight prick at his conscience. But instead of being bothered, he liked the reminder that the truth was important to him.

The constable led them toward the Money Pit. It seemed natural that he was in charge—he was the one in uniform. They emerged in the clearing and Jonah froze.

Another dead rabbit.

Marshall stared at the creature blankly, still fingering his chain. Sam Cooke began to whistle an unfamiliar tune.

"How long do we have?" Jonah said. "I'd like to walk around a bit. I haven't seen much of the island."

"An hour," Deacon said briskly. He grabbed the rabbit by the foot and tossed it near a wild rosebush.

Jonah couldn't help watching the brown fur land with a broken thud near another deteriorated mound of flesh and bones. The missing dead one from a few weeks ago. What was killing the rabbits?

Not wanting to lose his way, he ducked into the forest on what appeared to be an ancient path. In all of his trips to the island, he'd seen spruce trees, birch, and a few maples.

No oaks.

He found a sunny spot in a clearing and untied his backpack to take out the shovel. Digging three small holes several feet apart, he planted the oak seedlings he'd wrapped carefully and brought with him.

Reading *The Saturday Evening Post* article had reminded Jonah about the legend of Oak Island and how the treasure would surface once all of the oak trees were gone. The prospect of riches that had once thrilled him were now tarnished.

He planted three trees—one for Caleb, one for Charlotte, and one for Beaz.

Easily finding his way back to the Money Pit clearing, Jonah silently stopped beside the wild rosebush at the sight of Marshall standing alone on the timbers above the shaft. Light flashed as the golden chain snaked its way from Marshall's hand and slithered into the pit.

Evidence.

Gone.

Marshall spun around. "I've been wanting to put it back for months," he stuttered. "But I lost it for a little while."

Months? Charlotte had had the chain until just a few weeks ago. But why hadn't Marshall put it back at the same time he'd thrown the locket into the shaft?

"It's time to be going," Sam Cooke called out from the other side of the clearing. "Deacon's started the motor."

Flies buzzed on the dead rabbits, both tossed to the same spot. Jonah stared. The same spot. By the same person—Deacon? Was Marshall telling the truth about not being on the island for two years?

Then how did he know about the locket being in the Money Pit?

Evidence.

Blurred.

CHAPTER 29

ABRAHAM MORGAN AGREED—IT COULD HAVE been Deacon who'd thrown the locket into the shaft. What were the odds that two dead rabbits would be randomly discarded beside the same rosebush? The waters were muddied. Did Deacon cover for Marshall or did Marshall cover for Deacon?

As Jonah and his father suspected, Marshall's anonymous note never surfaced again to help direct suspicion away from Mr. Steevens, but an eyewitness finally came forward—Jacob Plant.

He and his brother, John, had left to work on their uncle's farm before news of Charlotte's disappearance had exploded across Western Shore. The farm was in a remote area of New Brunswick, and had no telephone. Only now, at the end of August, when he returned home, did Jacob learn he held the key to Mr. Steevens' absolution—he had seen Charlotte get out of the teacher's car and walk across the street to the general store.

Jacob wasn't sure, but he thought Charlotte had stopped to talk with someone. Possibly Marshall?

Deacon Delray wrapped up his investigation with surprising speed. "Not enough evidence to hold the teacher and no viable new suspects," he reported to the community who had crammed into the schoolhouse once again. And then he, Constable Deacon Delray, adjourned the meeting by announcing his resignation.

The rush of tourists died down and Western Shore mothers reverted to keeping an extra watch on their daughters—a monster was loose, unnamed and faceless, but a monster nonetheless.

But there were whispers.

And treasure hunters.

"They're dragging more drilling equipment over there," Beaz said. According to the doctor, the jagged scar across Beaz's forehead was healing nicely, but he hadn't smiled once since the incident.

Marshall and Deacon Delray lifted together, shoving a heavy wooden crate off the wharf and into the streamlined speedboat bound for Oak Island.

"Dad says this new conglomerate is throwing around money like they print it themselves." Jonah nodded at the brothers, now both working for the latest crop of treasure hunters. "And according to Ruth MacDonald, those two are making off like bandits, they're being paid so well."

Beaz said nothing and Jonah cast out his fishing line again. Maybe the old Beaz would have cracked a joke about the Delray brothers being murderers as well as bandits.

Maybe not.

There was no humour buried in this tragedy.

"Your Aunt Joyce seems nice," Jonah said.

"Yup," Beaz mumbled.

"She's your Dad's sister, right?"

"Yup."

Come back, Beaz.

"It's a fine day to watch the goings on," Sam Cooke said, sitting down beside them with his own reel. "Anything biting?"

"Not much," Jonah said, nodding toward the boat skimming over the waves to Oak Island. "Heard them say they're almost thirty feet down in a new shaft they're digging."

"That so?" The Wharf Prophet loaded bait on his hook. "I might sail down Yarmouth way. See some family over the Labour Day weekend. I haven't been back in ten years. Thought they might have a hankering for my pickled eggs."

"Oh?" Jonah said, again surprised that Sam Cooke was confiding personal details to him. A kid.

"Been wantin' to for a while, but I was waiting for all this murder business to get settled first."

"Well, it ain't," Beaz said. "So I guess you figured you better get going anyway." His voice sounded hollow, like all the stuffing had been scooped out of him and only a thin shell remained.

"But *we* know what really happened," Jonah said.

"What good does it do, the knowing? Charlotte's still dead and Marshall and Deacon still strut around like they own Western Shore." Beaz snapped his fishing rod out of the water.

His friend's anger wasn't all for the Delrays, Jonah knew. Somehow a murderous bully and a suspect cop made an easier target for raw emotions than the bare truth—Beaz's own mother had nearly killed him.

"Justice has a way of catching up with folks," the Wharf Prophet said.

It's true, Jonah thought. He felt ensnared in a punishment of his own making. Glancing sideways at a sombre Beaz, he wished for the millionth time that he'd told the truth earlier.

Quietly they fished all morning—baiting, casting, and reeling back in—only the Wharf Prophet had a growing pile of mackerel to show for his efforts. All the while, the old fisherman whistled "Merrily, We Roll Along."

"Come on, Beaz, let's get a pop," Jonah said as the noon sun shared its late August heat. Not as sultry as July, but warm enough to warrant a trip to the general store.

Betty Schofield's cooler was stacked full of icy drinks. "Here's your three cents change," she said with a sigh as she dropped Jonah's dime into the cash register.

On the surface it seemed that everything had circled back, but it hadn't.

Mrs. Hodder was gone.

Mr. Steevens was gone.

Charlotte was dead.

Marshall was...

The phone jangled and Betty's noisy bangles sliding down her bony arms added to the musical show. "Hello," she said, snapping her gum.

Gas escaped in a familiar puff as Jonah flipped the lid off his pop. This summer had left him with only simple joys—his family, his friend, and the sticky sweetness of his favourite drink costing seven cents again.

"Upon my soul!" Betty's shrill voice cried. "I'm going right over to set up my canteen. How many are dead?"

Jonah spun around in time to see Betty Schofield do the unthinkable.

She kicked off her high heels and jammed her feet into a pair of rubber boots.

EPILOGUE

ENGINEERS FROM HALIFAX WERE CALLED TO give evidence during the investigation into the Oak Island tragedy of 1958. The collapse of the newly dug shaft had claimed the lives of two men: Deacon Delray and his younger brother, Marshall.

Betty Schofield upped the price of pop back to a dime and this time decided to keep it there as the mild autumn weather drew curiosity seekers from near and far to the hallowed hamlet of Western Shore.

After a leisurely trip to Yarmouth, the Wharf Prophet returned and offered boat tours around the bay, giving visitors an opportunity to snap photographs of the legendary Oak Island for a small fee. Ruth MacDonald was his first customer, and Sam Cooke gave her a healthy shock when he informed her that the ride was on the house.

The community had weathered its worst summer storm and hottest summer day in many decades. It had also weathered another kind of element—suspicion.

But for some reason, unknown to most, after the island tragedy the air cleared. Daughters were free to roam—within reason, of course.

The Gold River–Western Shore Consolidated School opened its doors on the Wednesday after Labour Day. The newly assigned constable and a magnificently coiffed Betty Schofield held the scissors together as they cut the red ribbon at the ceremony. There were rumours of a budding romance and that he might become lucky husband number four.

Abraham Morgan went back to helping his clients plan their estates and buy and sell properties. Muriel alternated between baking dozens of cookies and sewing frilly baby things for the new nursery taking shape in Caleb's old bedroom.

But the island tragedy did not end Jonah's anxiety about the consequences of the summer of 1958. It wasn't guilt about planting the trees. Legend or not, he didn't believe that three little oak seedlings could have caused the shaft to collapse.

It was because of Beaz that Jonah's stomach stayed cinched in knots all through September and partway into October.

Finally, the cold grip of fear slipped away on Thanksgiving Day in the early afternoon, during a turkey dinner with all the trimmings that Jonah's family shared with Mr. Hodder, Aunt Joyce, and Beaz.

"I have news," Mr. Hodder said, clearing his throat as the pumpkin pie was being served.

"What? Is it...M—" Beaz's voice faltered.

"The chickens," Mr. Hodder said. "The captain is buying the whole lot. He said Jonah gave him the idea."

"Really?" Beaz picked up the dessert fork and gazed at his reflection in the handle.

Abandoning his own pie, and racing to the kitchen, Jonah checked time—twenty-two minutes past two o'clock.

"Golden," he whispered.

Now he would always remember the exact moment when Beaz smiled again.

ACKNOWLEDGMENTS

HAVE WE LOST AN AIR OF INNOCENCE FROM years past, or did we hide our darkness more successfully? Setting *Oak Island Revenge* in 1958 afforded me a glimpse into the childhood era of my parents. Perhaps it was a simpler time or perhaps simply a silenced time. Even today, with all of our modern modes of communication, some voices still remain unheard.

This story and its characters are fictional (as are the jail, the Chester gas station, and the location of the schoolhouse). However, little tidbits of truth, like a seven-cent bottle of pop in a general store, the opening of a new school in Gold River, and snippets of Oak Island treasure-hunting lore, help ground the mid-twentieth-century setting of Western Shore.

I am thankful to those who have supported me in the adventure of writing: Mom, Dad, Jo Ann, Daphne, Janet, Chad, Mark, Adele, Maxine, Beth, Joyce, Ruth, and Joan. Also, thanks to my fellow M.Ed. graduates for your encouragement—you ladies rock!

It has been my joy to work with Penelope and Patrick at Nimbus Publishing. I am grateful that you have helped bring Jonah and Beaz to life.

Finally, and most importantly, I acknowledge my family and my faith in God. Without these treasures, I would be a lonely soul searching for a home. Matthew, Joshua, and Elianna, your love helps me believe in miracles.